That night, when  for dinner, Jessica make her announce

"Have you heard t is sponsoring a Miss Teen Sweet Valley beauty pageant this year?" she asked innocently.

Elizabeth looked up. "That's what I was going to ask."

"I've entered," Jessica blurted out, at the precise moment Elizabeth said, "I'm organizing a protest committee."

Elizabeth stared at her sister in horror. "You're *entering*?" She folded her napkin and set it aside. "I don't believe it. Beauty pageants are demeaning to women. They should be outlawed."

"Outlawed?" Jessica protested. "*Demeaning?* Now, wait a minute. How can being chosen prettiest, smartest, and most talented be demeaning?"

"You think parading up and down a runway in a bathing suit and high heels is dignified?" Elizabeth asked sarcastically.

Jessica glared at her sister and then pushed back her chair as if to leave the table. But she couldn't quite bring herself to leave without having the final word. "If you ruin this for me, Elizabeth Wakefield, I'll never forgive you."

"If I have anything to say about it," Elizabeth answered coolly, "there won't be a beauty pageant in Sweet Valley. Not this year, not next year, not ever."

Bantam Books in the Sweet Valley High series
Ask your bookseller for the books you have missed

FRANCINE PASCAL'S

# SWEET VALLEY High

# MISS TEEN SWEET VALLEY

### Written by
## Kate William

### Created by
## FRANCINE PASCAL

BANTAM BOOKS
NEW YORK · TORONTO · LONDON · SYDNEY · AUCKLAND

RL 6, age 12 and up

MISS TEEN SWEET VALLEY
*A Bantam Book / June 1991*

*Produced by Daniel Weiss Associates, Inc.*
*33 West 17th Street*
*New York, NY 10011*

*Cover art by James Mathewuse*

ISBN 0-553-29060-6

*Published simultaneously in the United States and Canada*

PRINTED IN THE UNITED STATES OF AMERICA

OPM     0 9 8 7 6 5 4 3 2 1

*To Amy Ellen Dyson*

# One

Jessica Wakefield leaned forward to study her reflection in the mirror over the bathroom sink. Her identical twin sister, Elizabeth, stood beside her, arms folded, watching with a grin.

"See any wrinkles?" Elizabeth teased.

Jessica was not amused. For the first time in a long while, she doubted the appeal of the face and figure gazing back at her. Like Elizabeth, she was a perfect size six, with wavy blond hair bleached by the sun, and sparkling blue-green eyes. Each girl had a glamorous California tan and a dimple in her left cheek. Even their voices were alike, as was the way they laughed.

But the similarities ended there, however, because when it came to their personalities, the twins were very different.

1

Elizabeth liked to read, and loved writing her column for the school paper, *The Oracle*. She spent most of her free time with her best friend, Enid Rollins, or her boyfriend, Todd Wilkins. Still, Elizabeth was popular at Sweet Valley High, and the teachers liked her as much as the students did.

Jessica was a whirlwind of energy, with a whole different set of friends, and she liked to travel in a slightly faster lane. Because she hated being bored, she was always trying new things, and the exact center of attention was her favorite place to be. She didn't understand why Elizabeth would rather hang around with one guy all the time instead of playing the field and dating lots of different guys.

"Do you think I'm losing my looks?" Jessica asked, turning her head to one side and then the other to study her profile from both directions.

Elizabeth smiled and shook her head as if she found the question too ridiculous to even answer. "Todd and I are going to study at the library," she said. "See you later."

Jessica sighed and stepped back to check herself out from a little distance. She frowned. The mirror told her that she looked as good as ever, but when Steven, her older brother, brought college friends home, they didn't seem to know she was alive. What was wrong with her?

2

No closer to an answer than she had been before, Jessica went into her room, which was linked with Elizabeth's by the bathroom they shared, and sat cross-legged on the bed.

The weekend before, some of Steven's crowd had visited the Wakefields. Jessica had been particularly attracted to an especially cute guy named Frazer McConnell. And although she had used all of her considerable skill flirting with him, Frazer hadn't even noticed her.

She cupped her chin in one hand and sighed again. The guys at Sweet Valley High seemed to be as fascinated by her as ever, but Jessica was tired of immature boys. How was she supposed to date college men like Frazer McConnell if she couldn't even get them to *look* at her?

Jessica fell backward onto the mattress and stared up at the ceiling. She was slipping, and she had to do something about it. But what?

Because everyone else in the family was out, Jessica had the house to herself that evening. Two different guys had called, both Sweet Valley High seniors. One had wanted to take her to the movies, the other to a beach party. But Jessica had turned both offers down. She had told herself she'd rather stay home than date a kid.

Having seen what boring shows were on TV,

though, she was beginning to have second thoughts. Moping around the house was not Jessica's style.

Jessica sank into her dad's favorite chair and glanced at the copy of the *Sweet Valley News* that was lying on the floor. The word *prizes* leaped out at her from a headline.

Her heart beating faster, Jessica snatched up the newspaper. Her aquamarine eyes widened as she read the short article describing the beauty pageant planned by the Sweet Valley Chamber of Commerce. Their goal was to raise money for a new community pool.

Jessica had already heard about the contest and had even decided she would enter. But she'd had so many things on her mind lately, including Frazer McConnell, that she'd completely forgotten about it.

Eagerly, Jessica reread the short newspaper piece. Some lucky girl between the ages of fifteen and eighteen would be named Miss Teen Sweet Valley. There would be a cash award, and various local merchants had agreed to donate "wonderful" prizes. The event would be held three weeks from that coming Saturday in the auditorium at Sweet Valley High.

*"Yes!"* Jessica yelled to the empty house. She leapt from the chair in her excitement and waved the newspaper. She smiled to the invisible audience in the room, raised her hands high

over her head, and whooped, "And the winner is . . . *Jessica Wakefield!*"

Jessica imagined herself standing in a circle of golden light on the stage of the auditorium at Sweet Valley High while a fur-trimmed velvet cape was draped over her shoulders and a gleaming crown was placed on her head. The master of ceremonies laid two dozen red roses in her arms, and in that moment the fantasy was so real that Jessica could almost smell the flowers.

Jessica pictured herself gliding triumphantly down the makeshift runway, waving one elegant, gloved hand at the adoring audience, her eyes glistening with endearing tears. Cheers and applause filled her ears and she could see people nodding to one another, approving the judges' choice. Everyone agreed that it had been no contest; Jessica Wakefield had been the obvious winner from the first.

After the pageant, she would surely appear on TV, and this time Elizabeth wouldn't have to stand in for her, as she had the time Jessica won a spot on Eric Parker's talk show. Who knew what might happen once the publicity started picking up speed? Movie and modeling contracts would surely come her way. She would become rich and famous.

A sharp pain in her shin brought Jessica back from dreamland in a hurry. She'd walked right into the edge of the coffee table. But even that small mishap couldn't dim her excitement, because she'd found the solution to her boy problem. She would win the contest—there was no question of her not winning—and when she did, Frazer and a lot of other college guys would be *begging* her for dates.

What guy in his right mind could resist Miss Teen Sweet Valley?

Although she'd been so excited all night that she had hardly been able to sleep, Jessica didn't mention the beauty pageant to her family at breakfast the next morning. Later, at school, she was glad she hadn't been the one to bring it up with her friends, either. It was hard to keep her intention of entering, and winning, to herself. But it was better to wait and see who else was signing up in order to evaluate her competition. If the other candidates knew Jessica was entering, they were bound to get discouraged and withdraw. In that case, either the pageant would be canceled or Jessica would win simply because she was the only person in the contest.

Would she still get the prizes, she wondered, if that happened?

The thing to do, she decided, was to play it

cool and pretend the pageant didn't matter much to her one way or the other.

At lunchtime, Jessica joined Amy Sutton and Lila Fowler at their usual table in the cafeteria. Her friends were chattering about the contest.

"I've already lost interest in the whole silly idea," Lila Fowler said with a shrug. "I mean, a shopping spree? *Please.* I can already buy whatever I want, so why should I go to all the trouble of walking down a runway for a few dumb prizes?"

"The whole thing is probably fixed," Amy said with a toss of her sleek blond hair. "You can bet the judges will have already decided who the winner is before the pageant even starts."

Jessica suppressed a smile. She wouldn't go so far as to say the pageant was *fixed*, but she was fairly sure it was in the bag. One look at her and the judges would know she was born to be Miss Teen Sweet Valley.

A burst of laughter at a nearby table made Jessica, Amy, and Lila look around. Elizabeth and some of her friends, including Enid, Todd, and Maria Santelli, Winston Egbert's girlfriend and a member of the cheerleading squad, were talking about the pageant, too.

Todd's voice carried over the general din of the cafeteria. "Can you imagine the question-and-answer segment?"

"What solutions would you suggest for combatting the greenhouse effect?" Enid asked in a mock-serious voice.

Elizabeth answered in a silly, high-pitched tone, batting her long, thick lashes in the process. "I think the whole world should stop using hair spray and switch to mousse!"

The crowd at Elizabeth's table seemed to think the performance was pretty funny, but Jessica didn't crack a smile.

Then it was Todd's turn to be the questioner. "How can we feed the starving people of the world?" he asked in a deep, master-of-ceremonies voice.

This time Enid played the pageant entrant, giggling like an airhead. "Let them eat yogurt," she said with a flippant wave of one hand. "Or tofu!"

Before long her sister's game was attracting attention from all over the cafeteria, and Jessica felt a tingle of envy, as well as resentment. In her opinion, Elizabeth and the others were acting like snobs. Not all beauty pageant contestants were silly and uninformed. And what was wrong with wanting to win some great prizes and get some well-deserved attention at the same time?

By then the kids at Elizabeth's table were pretending to quiz an invisible contestant.

"What would you do if you were in charge of a frog-jumping competition and all the frogs got away?" Elizabeth offered.

"When you finish your seven years of junior college, what will you do with the rest of your life?" Maria put in, her dark eyes sparkling.

"Do your lips move when you read?" Todd inquired, raising his eyebrows. "Do you read at all? Can you spell 'book'?"

Jessica turned back to her lunch tray, but her appetite was gone and her cheeks were hot with indignation. She reached for her soda and took a big gulp.

"What's the matter?" Lila asked when she saw Jessica's red face.

Jessica just shrugged and said, "Nothing."

Amy smiled, seemingly oblivious to the antics at the other table. "I've heard the prizes are really great," she said, counting on her fingers as she began to name things the Chamber of Commerce would be awarding the pageant winner. "There's the shopping spree at Simple Splendor, that fantastic new boutique in the mall, a brass bed, a stereo, a thousand dollars in cash—"

Lila gave a bored sigh. "I heard it was five thousand," she said.

Lila had Jessica's full attention. Five thousand dollars? With that kind of money, Jessica could buy a terrific late-model used car, maybe a sleek silver foreign one. No more sharing the Fiat with Elizabeth!

"Hmmmm," she said.

"Yes," Amy said, as though making some final decision. "Barry's right. I'm definitely going to enter the pageant."

Jessica narrowed her eyes for a second, opened her mouth to protest, but changed her mind at the last second. Sure, Amy was drop-dead gorgeous, but she couldn't compete with Jessica when it came to talent and personality. And she was nowhere near Jessica in the maturity department, even though since Amy had started working at Project Youth she had actually been acting more responsibly. "I think that's a good idea," Jessica said graciously.

Lila looked skeptical. "What would you do for the talent segment?" she asked Amy.

Amy was baffled. "Well, I . . ."

A talent. Jessica's mind whirred. She was a good dancer. She and Bruce Patman had won a contest once, and she had even studied ballet and modern dance for a while.

No problem.

"I could twirl my baton," Amy said triumphantly.

Jessica smiled to herself. So much the better. Amy's baton twirling wasn't going to impress anybody. She'd been good once, but she was out of practice now. An original dance performance, on the other hand, would set the judges back on their heels. "I think that's what you should do," she told Amy. "Twirl your baton."

Lila stood up, holding her lunch tray in both hands. She looked down at Amy with a sort of indulgent pity in her eyes. "You wouldn't catch *me* making a fool of myself in front of half of Sweet Valley," she said.

Amy blushed a little, but didn't answer. Jessica wondered why Lila didn't go and sit with Elizabeth and the others if she was so opposed to beauty pageants.

"See you later," Jessica said, and Lila walked away.

Amy bit her lower lip for a moment, then blurted out, "Do you think it's silly of me to enter this pageant, Jess? Barry thinks I should go for it. But, well, maybe I should forget the whole thing."

Jessica was certain Amy would lose, and she felt a pang of remorse when she smiled and said, "I think Barry's right. You should enter."

Amy's smile brightened, and she and Jessica returned their lunch trays and left the cafeteria together. They were standing in front of Jessica's locker when Cara Walker, a fellow cheerleader, appeared.

"I guess you've heard about the pageant," she said.

Jessica closed her locker door. "We've heard," she said thoughtfully. Cara was dating Jessica's brother, Steven. Jessica wondered why her friend could attract a college guy and she couldn't.

"Are you entering?" Amy asked.

Cara shrugged. "I don't know. How about you?" she asked both Jessica and Amy.

"Definitely," Amy answered.

"Who knows?" Jessica replied with an off-hand shrug. She tried her best to look uninterested but the truth was, she was going to have trouble concentrating on her history quiz. Daydreams about driving around Sweet Valley in her own fantastic silver car were crowding her mind.

Amy looked curiously at Jessica, but before she could say anything the bell rang and Jessica hurried off to class.

That evening after dinner Jessica piled all her swimsuits on her bed and began to sort through them. Even though she was confident she'd win the title of Miss Teen Sweet Valley, the swimsuit competition was important and there would be no harm in looking her best.

A knock at the door linking Jessica's room to the bathroom made her mutter a distracted "Come in."

Elizabeth entered and glanced at the colorful pile of suits in the middle of Jessica's bed. "Is there a big beach party coming up that I don't know about?" she asked.

Jessica shook her head. She held up a pink-

and-gray striped suit and gazed at her reflection in the mirror. "Just sorting through things," she answered without looking at her sister. After the way Elizabeth and her friends had joked about the pageant that day at lunch, Jessica was even less eager to talk about her plans than she had been before.

The suit was French cut, and while it never failed to drive the guys at the beach crazy, it might cause a problem if the pageant judges turned out to be middle-aged conservatives. She reached for a black one-piece, but it was pretty sexy, too.

Jessica sighed and at last looked at her sister. "I don't suppose I could borrow a suit from you? Maybe that plain turquoise one you bought last week?"

Elizabeth's expression was thoughtful, but she shrugged. "Sure," she agreed. "Why not?" Then she went back to her room to get the swimsuit.

It was perfect, Jessica thought later as she stood in front of the mirror. Not too ordinary, not too sexy.

A smile curved her lips. She could almost feel the weight of that glittering crown, the warmth of the spotlight. She lifted a bottle of hair spray in a sort of toast. "Here's to the first Miss Teen Sweet Valley," she said.

# Two

Jessica was lying on a deck chair beside the Wakefields' pool, soaking up the bright Saturday sunshine and dreaming as her golden tan deepened.

The more she thought about the pageant, the more excited she became. She was determined to win, to show Frazer McConnell and every other great-looking college guy in Sweet Valley just what he'd been missing. And the prizes! She could spend hours imagining herself on a shopping spree at Simple Splendor or driving that special someone to the beach in her silver convertible sports car.

Jessica expected the talent segment to be the toughest part of the contest, but her dancing would wrap that up for her. All she had to do was pick out the music, work up a routine, and make sure she looked absolutely great in her costume.

Jessica sat up to rub suntan oil onto her shapely legs, then lay back down and let her imagination roam. A few minutes later a loud splash interrupted her thoughts. Jessica raised herself on her elbows to see Steven and *Frazer McConnell.*

"Hi, Jess," Steven said, surfacing on the other side of the sparkling blue-green water and tossing his head to shake the water from his face. Steven had been spending a lot of time at home lately, partly because it was easier to see Cara and partly because he was working on a special project and needed a quiet place to study. According to Steven, the dorm was a zoo.

Jessica was uncomfortably aware that Frazer, who had sun-bleached blond hair, broad shoulders, expressive brown eyes, and skin bronzed by days at the beach, didn't seem to notice that she looked fantastic in her black two-piece suit. When he said hi, he might have been talking to the patio furniture for all the interest he showed.

Jessica's heart took a dip, then soared again. There was no reason to worry. Once she'd landed the Miss Teen Sweet Valley title, Frazer would never ignore her again. Settling back to resume her sunbathing, Jessica tried to appear bored and uninterested, but her pulse was pounding. She watched through her thick lashes as Steven and his friend enjoyed their morning swim.

Snatches of conversation reached her ears as the guys left the pool and began drying themselves off with towels they'd brought from the house.

"Cara and I are going out for pizza and a movie tonight," Steven said to his friend. "Why don't you call Monica Crane or somebody and come with us?"

Jessica felt a sting. She wondered about Monica Crane, and what it was about her that put her in the running for a date with a hunk like Frazer.

"Can't," Frazer answered, his muscles rippling as he towel-dried his hair, then his arms and shoulders. "My kid sister has a dance recital, and I promised I'd be there."

He spoke with a sort of quiet pride. Jessica's attention, already focused on Frazer, was intensified, like sunlight shining through a magnifying glass.

Steven was already headed toward the patio doors. "That's great," he said, though Jessica suspected he wasn't really any more interested in the things Frazer's younger sister did than Frazer was in Jessica and Elizabeth's activities. "What kind of dancing does she do?"

"Modern," Frazer said just before he and Steven disappeared into the house. And in that moment, Jessica's choice of modern dance for her talent number became definite. Now, not only would her dancing impress the judges, it would impress Frazer, too. He seemed proud of his sister's accomplishments, and the fact that Jessica had something important in common with her *had* to work in her favor.

Jessica turned onto her stomach, rested her cheek on her hands, and dozed off. She dreamed she was walking into the Dairi Burger hand in hand with Frazer McConnell. She looked terrific in a glamorous evening gown and the winner's sash, the Miss Teen Sweet Valley crown gleaming on her head. In her free arm she carried a huge bouquet of roses.

Elizabeth Wakefield's normally even temper simmered that following Monday morning when she and Enid arrived at school and found the hallway walls practically papered in announcements about the upcoming beauty pageant.

"They're really going to do it," Elizabeth muttered, shaking her head. "They're going to hold that silly, sexist contest right here at Sweet Valley High, in our own auditorium!"

Enid sighed and shrugged. "I plan to ignore the whole thing."

Elizabeth opened her locker door and hung

17

her shoulder bag on the hook inside. "Sometimes you have to stand up for what you believe in," she said quietly. "You can't just sit back and let things happen."

"I suppose you're right," Enid answered. "So what do you plan to do?"

Elizabeth had already asked herself that question. In fact, she'd been thinking about it all weekend: while she and Todd swam at the beach, while they played miniature golf on Friday night, and even while they watched movies at Todd's on Saturday. "We'll organize a protest committee," she said decisively as she and Enid entered their first class of the day. "I'll write an article for *The Oracle*, too, about how beauty contests exploit women."

Just then Todd came into the classroom. He followed the girls to their seats and sat down next to Elizabeth.

"What exploits women?" he asked.

"Beauty pageants do," Elizabeth answered with conviction. Even as she spoke, her ideas were gathering steam. "They focus on all the wrong things, too. How a person looks instead of who she is and how she—"

Todd grinned and held up both hands in comical surrender. "You don't have to convince me, Liz. I'm on your side."

The room was filling up with other students,

and a lot of the girls were talking about the pageant.

"We'll go to the mall and the library," Elizabeth announced decisively, "and collect signatures protesting the use of the school auditorium—which, of course, belongs to the taxpayers—for such a ridiculous purpose. And we'll get the students and teachers at Sweet Valley High to sign."

"The people speak," Todd said with a grin.

Elizabeth had a hard time keeping her mind on classwork that day, and right after school she hurried to *The Oracle* office. She was sitting at her desk, making notes for the article she planned to write, when she looked up and saw Dana Larson and Olivia Davidson standing in front of her, smiling.

Dana was an unconventional type, the lead singer of Sweet Valley High's popular rock band, The Droids. Olivia was a talented painter who also handled the arts column for *The Oracle*.

"She's got that *look* about her," Dana said.

Olivia folded her arms and pretended to study Elizabeth seriously. "Yes," she agreed. "I'd know the Liz-on-the-warpath look anywhere. She's preparing to do journalistic battle."

Elizabeth grinned and spread her hands. "You caught me. What can I say?"

Dana perched on the edge of Elizabeth's

desk. "You can tell us which cause has you so worked up."

"It's that beauty pageant the Chamber of Commerce is holding," Elizabeth answered, her smile fading away to an annoyed frown. "It's bad enough that they're sponsoring the thing at all, but to drag all of Sweet Valley High into it by using our auditorium . . . well, it just really bugs me."

"I agree," Olivia said. She pulled up a chair and pushed graceful, artistic fingers through her curly brown hair. "The statement it makes is totally wrong."

Dana nodded. "You've got my support too, Liz."

"Great," Elizabeth said. "Let's try to get some other student volunteers to collect signatures on a petition."

"We could march in front of the courthouse," Olivia suggested, and Elizabeth knew her friend was already designing picket signs in her mind.

"And the supermarket," Dana added.

"And the library," Elizabeth put in.

With that the protest committee was born, and Elizabeth Wakefield was in her element—planning, organizing, directing. If she had anything to say about it, the pageant would be called off and the dignity of Sweet Valley womanhood would be preserved.

*   *   *

Lively music filled the boutique, making the walls and ceiling of the dressing room vibrate. Jessica hummed along as she admired the way the white leotard and tights she was wearing emphasized her suntan.

She had to admit it, she looked gorgeous. She smiled at her image, then hastily changed back into jeans and a white ruffled camisole. Buying the outfit would mean parting with a major chunk of her allowance, but Jessica reasoned that a woman had to be willing to make investments in her future.

After carefully combing her hair and touching up her lip gloss, Jessica came out of the dressing room, paid the clerk, and left the shop. She crossed the mall's wide concourse to Simple Splendor, where she spent an hour and a half going through the racks and trying things on. Once she'd decided which outfits she was going to choose on her shopping spree, she smiled charmingly at the baffled saleswoman and set out for the parking lot.

She was so happy and excited that it seemed her feet were barely skimming the asphalt. In just a few weeks she would be the envy of every girl at Sweet Valley High.

It was a very warm day, and Steven's car was in the driveway again when Jessica arrived home. Maybe he'd brought Frazer with him and they were taking a swim even now.

Mrs. Wakefield was tearing spinach leaves for a salad when Jessica entered the kitchen a minute or two later. Jessica was disappointed that there had been no sign of Frazer when she looked out at the pool.

"Hi, honey," Alice Wakefield said, glancing at the shopping bag in Jessica's hand. "Buy something new?"

Jessica nodded. She would announce her participation in the beauty pageant when the moment was exactly right, and not a minute before. "Nothing spectacular," she said.

Mrs. Wakefield reached for a colander full of tomatoes and began to slice them into juicy wedges. "Elizabeth will be late for dinner. She's working on some project for *The Oracle*. But Steven brought Frazer home with him, so we'll still need five place settings. Would you take care of setting the table, please?"

Jessica smiled brightly. "Sure," she agreed with uncharacteristic readiness. "I'll just put this bag in my room, then I'll be right down."

Mrs. Wakefield looked a little surprised at Jessica's willingness to help out, but she recovered quickly. She reached for a cucumber to slice and said, "Good."

As Jessica passed Steven's room she heard the stereo blaring, and grinned. Frazer didn't

22

know it yet, but in a matter of weeks he was going to be absolutely crazy about her.

By the time Elizabeth got home from her long meeting with Penny Ayala, editor-in-chief of *The Oracle*, Todd, Enid, Dana, Olivia, Maria, and Winston, dinner was over, the dishwasher was whirring away, and the whole family had gone their separate ways.

Her dad, a partner in a prominent law firm, was in his study going over some notes for a case, and she found her mother upstairs in the master bedroom studying drawings of a new design project. Jessica was shut up in her room, music pounding against the door as if it were trying to escape.

Elizabeth felt a headache coming on, but when she stepped into her own room she felt a little better. It was quiet, tastefully decorated, and impeccably neat.

She set her notebook down on the square table that served as a desk. Hearing a series of thumps from Jessica's room even louder than the throb of the music, she frowned and went through the bathroom to knock at her sister's door.

"Jess?"

There was no answer. Little wonder, Elizabeth thought. The stereo was playing at a decibel level that would raise the dead. Elizabeth opened the door and stepped into her sister's room.

Jessica was standing in the middle of her bedroom floor which, as always, was littered with clothes, towels, and books. She was wearing a white dance outfit and moving expressively to the music. Actually, she looked pretty graceful, and although Elizabeth wondered what her sister was doing, she was too tired to pursue the matter. Besides, she felt like a spy standing there.

Elizabeth slipped back out and returned to her own room to write a long entry in her journal.

As soon as her last class let out the next afternoon, Jessica hurried to the parking lot and slid behind the wheel of the red Fiat Spider she shared with Elizabeth.

She started the engine, put the small car in gear, and headed for downtown Sweet Valley. She passed the courthouse and pulled to a stop in front of the small building that housed the Chamber of Commerce. She pulled the keys from the ignition and dropped them into her purse.

After checking her hair and lip gloss in the rearview mirror, Jessica got out of the car and went inside the building.

"I'm here to sign up for the beauty pageant,"

she told the receptionist, who greeted her with a smile.

The woman had her pegged for a sure winner, Jessica could tell.

"Just fill this out, please," said the receptionist. She handed Jessica a couple of forms, a pen, and a clipboard. "We'll need a black-and-white photograph for the newspaper, and there is a small entry fee. Oh, and one of your parents will need to sign a permission slip."

Jessica nodded. She hoped the entry fee wouldn't be beyond her somewhat limited means. Jessica walked over to a folding chair against the wall and sat down to fill out the main form. She would return later with the signed permission slip and the black-and-white photograph. She would ask Lila to take the picture with her fancy camera. Elizabeth was into photography and had recently joined the photography club, but Jessica preferred not to tell her sister why she wanted her picture taken. Not yet, anyway.

As it happened, Jessica had the amount of money required for the entry fee, and when she left the Chamber of Commerce's offices that afternoon she was well on her way to being officially entered in the Miss Teen Sweet Valley contest. The permission slip, along with a sheaf of papers listing the rules and regulations of the pageant, were stuffed into her purse.

When Jessica got home Elizabeth was in the kitchen taking her turn at fixing dinner. Jessica was tempted to share the news of her imminent reign over Sweet Valley, but memories of Elizabeth's disparaging comments in the cafeteria stopped her. She was keeping her entry in the pageant from her friends for strategic purposes, to throw them off guard. And for a while longer she would keep her entry a secret from Elizabeth, too. Her sister would find out soon enough.

"Hi, Liz," she said, almost sighing the words. "What's for dinner?"

"Grilled chicken," Elizabeth answered with her usual smile. She looked a little tired to Jessica, and maybe a bit worried, too. But because Jessica had preoccupations of her own, she didn't ask about Elizabeth's.

"Ummm," Jessica replied. "Sounds terrific."

At dinner Mr. Wakefield talked about his current case, and Mrs. Wakefield described a new design project she and her partner, Doug, were working on. Steven finished his food, carried his plate back to the kitchen, and went off to spend some time with Cara. Elizabeth ate quietly. She seemed to have something serious on her mind.

Jessica decided it wasn't quite the time to spring the good news on her family.

# Three

At school the next day everybody was talking about Elizabeth's campaign to stop the Chamber of Commerce from sponsoring the beauty pageant. Jessica was annoyed, but not worried. She was *destined* to be Miss Teen Sweet Valley; she could feel it in her blood.

That night when the Wakefields gathered for dinner, Elizabeth was in a thoughtful mood.

In spite of Elizabeth's feelings regarding the beauty pageant, Jessica decided it was time to make the announcement. After all, she was almost an official contestant. She'd done the really important footwork, like signing up for the pageant, buying the leotard and tights, and deciding on the music for her dance. Besides, she couldn't keep her participation a secret forever. She needed one of her parents' signatures on the permission slip.

"Have you heard that the Chamber of Commerce is choosing a Miss Teen Sweet Valley this year?" she asked innocently, smiling to herself because she knew just how Elizabeth was going to react.

Elizabeth looked up. "That's what I was going to ask."

"I've entered," Jessica blurted out at the precise moment Elizabeth said, "I'm organizing a protest committee."

Elizabeth stared at her sister in horror. "You're *entering?*"

"Everybody take cover," Steven put in with a grin, "here comes the fallout."

Elizabeth folded her table napkin and set it aside. "I don't believe it," she said, and Jessica knew by her tone that she was making an effort to speak calmly. "Beauty pageants are demeaning to women. They should be outlawed."

"Outlawed?" Jessica protested. *"Demeaning?* Now, wait a minute. How can being chosen prettiest, smartest, and most talented be demeaning?"

"You think parading up and down a runway in a bathing suit and high heels is dignified?" Elizabeth asked sarcastically.

Mr. Wakefield cleared his throat. "Just a minute, girls," he said quietly. "You each have a right to your own opinion."

Jessica glared at her sister. It wasn't the first time she and Elizabeth had been on opposite sides of a controversy. In fact, because their outlooks on life were so different, it happened often. But something about Elizabeth's attitude stung. Jessica felt put down, like she had in the cafeteria when Elizabeth's friends were mocking beauty pageant contestants.

"I don't think I'm hungry anymore," Jessica said in a chilly tone. "May I please be excused?"

Mrs. Wakefield nodded and exchanged a glance with her husband. Jessica pushed back her chair as if to leave the table.

But she couldn't quite bring herself to leave without having the final word. "If you ruin this for me, Elizabeth Wakefield, I'll never forgive you."

"If I have anything to say about it," Elizabeth answered coolly, "there won't be a beauty pageant in Sweet Valley. Not this year, not next year, not ever."

"Incoming mortar fire," Steven warned, amused.

Jessica knew there was no sense in arguing with Elizabeth while her twin was in such a stubborn state of mind. Jessica went to her room and closed the door hard behind her.

*    *    *

Elizabeth stopped a woman pushing a baby stroller through the crowded mall. "Excuse me," she said with a friendly smile. "I'm Elizabeth Wakefield, and I'd like to get your opinion on something."

The young mother returned Elizabeth's smile, but she looked tired. "Yes?"

Elizabeth offered the clipboard and pen she was holding. "My friends and I are collecting signatures to protest the use of the auditorium at Sweet Valley High for a beauty pageant." She indicated Penny, Olivia, Enid, Dana, and Claire Middleton, who were also stopping passers-by. "We think contests like this set women back a hundred years."

"I kind of enjoy watching pageants on TV," the woman said, pushing her wispy bangs back off her forehead with one hand.

"The question is," Elizabeth replied earnestly, "do we really want to encourage the idea that looks are the most important quality a woman can have? What about personal initiative? What about persistence, intelligence, skill?"

The baby in the stroller began to cry, and the young mother took the pen and clipboard from Elizabeth with a sigh. "You're right, I suppose," she said as she signed.

Elizabeth thanked her and turned to stop a

distinguished-looking businessman in a tailored suit.

"Excuse me, sir. . . ."

About fifteen minutes had passed when Amy Sutton appeared, walking hand in hand with her boyfriend, Barry Rork, a member of the Sweet Valley High tennis team.

They stopped to listen while Elizabeth gave her quick speech, and Amy looked annoyed when the grandmotherly type Elizabeth had been talking to signed the petition.

"What are you trying to do?" she demanded.

"I think it's obvious, Amy," Elizabeth replied politely. "We want the Chamber of Commerce to call off the pageant."

Amy's cheeks flushed. "Have you ever heard the saying, 'Live and let live'? Nobody's forcing you to attend the pageant. I just don't understand why you'd want to spoil it for everybody else."

"Amy . . ." Barry said hesitantly.

Amy ignored Barry. She folded her arms and frowned. "Well, you're not going to get *me* to sign!"

Elizabeth spoke quietly, and with a smile. "I didn't expect to, Amy. I take it you're planning to enter?"

"I already have," Amy answered with a defiant toss of her hair. "C'mon, Barry." She took Barry's arm and they walked away.

"Some things never change," Dana commented as she came over to stand beside Elizabeth.

Elizabeth sighed. "Actually," she said, "Amy *has* changed. You read my interview with her. She's doing some great work at Project Youth, taking calls from troubled kids. When it comes to beauty pageants, though, it looks as if she and I will never agree."

Elizabeth put Amy out of her mind and thought instead about her twin. Jessica's commitment to winning the pageant was just as strong as Elizabeth's commitment to stopping it. Elizabeth loved her sister, but that didn't stop them from being on opposing sides of an issue.

Later that night, after an awkward family dinner at which neither Jessica nor Elizabeth joined in the conversation, Elizabeth went to her room and rolled a piece of paper into the typewriter. Then, with quick keystrokes, she typed: "Why Beauty Pageants Should Be Outlawed."

Beneath the title she added, "by Elizabeth Wakefield."

After a glance at her notes and a few minutes spent organizing her thoughts, Elizabeth began to do what she did best: write. Words flowed from her mind onto the paper. She wrote one draft of the article, and then another.

When she laid the last page face down on the

table beside her typewriter, Elizabeth felt better. Maybe her opinions wouldn't be appreciated by some people—Jessica, for example—but she'd stated them clearly, and that was what a journalist was supposed to do.

On Friday afternoon Jessica dragged Lila to the mall the moment school was out.

"I have to look sensational for the pageant," Jessica said as she and Lila stalked through the mall.

"You *always* look sensational," Lila replied, sounding a little bored. "And how do you plan to buy new clothes when you just got through telling me you've spent all your allowance?"

"Part of being Miss Teen Sweet Valley," Jessica grinned, tapping her temple with one index finger, "is having brains. On the night of the pageant I'm going to wear the most beautiful evening gown I can find, and it won't cost a cent."

Lila's eyes widened. "Jess, you wouldn't shoplift!"

"Of course not," Jessica said pointedly. She hadn't forgotten how Lila had framed her for shoplifting, hoping to take Jessica's place on Eric Parker's talk show, and she wanted Lila to know she remembered. In the end Elizabeth had stepped in and saved the day by appearing in Jessica's place, pretending to *be* Jessica. As far as Lila knew, it had been Jessica on stage!

Lila's cheeks were tinged pink and she examined her beautifully manicured nails as she and Jessica entered Simple Splendor.

Normally, Jessica liked to look in every store in the mall before she chose an important outfit, but that day, the moment she entered Simple Splendor, the *perfect* dress was staring her in the face.

It was a pale pink creation with a full chiffon skirt. Tiny pearls stitched to the simple, fitted bodice gave it a look that made Jessica think of knights in shining armor going into battle for their ladies.

The dress was perfect for royalty.

Jessica's fingers trembled a little as she reached for the tag, and relief flooded her when she saw that the gown was a size six. She didn't bother to check the price; she didn't have any money. She didn't need any.

"Would you like to try it on?" asked the saleswoman, a well-dressed woman about Mrs. Wakefield's age.

Jessica slipped into the dressing room and put on the dress. When she saw herself in the mirror she had an odd, enchanted feeling, as though a fairy godmother had touched her with a wand and turned her into a princess. All she needed now was a crown.

"You look wonderful," said the saleswoman as Jessica emerged.

Even Lila looked impressed, in an envious sort of way. "We're just browsing," she said.

Jessica turned to one side and admired her reflection. She could just see the winner's sash draped across the front of that fabulous dress.

"I'd like to wear it in the Miss Teen Sweet Valley pageant," she told the saleswoman, smiling her most dazzling smile. "Of course, it would say in the program that the dress came from Simple Splendor, and I could bring it back the very next day. In excellent condition, naturally."

The woman looked thoughtful. "I suppose that would be good publicity, wouldn't it?"

"The best," Jessica agreed quickly. When she came back to the mall for her shopping spree as Miss Teen Sweet Valley, of course, she would buy the gown outright.

"You certainly make an excellent model," the saleswoman said. "Let me call the manager."

Jessica turned her smile setting from "dazzle" to "sweet." "Thank you," she said in her warmest, most musical voice.

Five minutes later, Jessica and Lila left the store with the magical dress.

"Wow," Lila raved. "How did you do that?"

Jessica batted her eyelashes. "Do what?" she asked, teasing.

Lila laughed. "You have more nerve than anybody I know," she said with grudging admiration.

Jessica's happy mood dimmed a little, though, when she caught sight of Elizabeth and her crew in the mall's central concourse. Either they'd just arrived, or she hadn't noticed them on the way in.

"What are they up to?" Lila asked, following Jessica's troubled stare.

"Guess," Jessica answered with an angry sigh. "You know that Liz has decided that pageants are sexist. She's out to get the whole thing canceled."

Lila nodded. "That sounds like Liz. Looks like they're getting a lot of signatures, too."

Jessica shifted the bulky dress box to her other arm and started toward her sister.

"Hi," she said coolly, enjoying the startled expression in Elizabeth's eyes when she looked up from her clipboard and saw Jessica standing in front of her.

"Care to sign?" Elizabeth asked mildly, without missing a beat. She held out the clipboard and a pen.

"Right," Jessica answered, ignoring both items.

Elizabeth stood her ground, her chin set at an obstinate angle, and said nothing.

"I suppose you're planning to keep this up all weekend," Jessica said when the silence became strained. She was talking about the anti-pageant campaign, of course, and she knew Elizabeth knew it.

Elizabeth nodded. "Until the Chamber of Commerce sees things our way and calls off the contest," she replied.

Jessica gave her twin a slow once-over. "Good luck," she said, without a shred of sincerity.

"Same to you," Elizabeth replied, with about the same amount of enthusiasm.

Enid touched Elizabeth's arm as Jessica walked away. "Don't worry," she scolded good-naturedly. "Things will be back to normal between you and Jessica as soon as this controversy blows over."

Elizabeth nodded, but inside she wasn't at all sure her best friend was right. By working to get the pageant called off she might win a moral victory, but she might also lose her only sister!

That night, in the Wakefields' basement, Elizabeth and her friends consumed three take-out pizzas while making signs with slogans like WOMEN ARE MORE THAN PRETTY FACES and NO MORE PAGEANTS. The march on the courthouse was planned for ten o'clock the next morning.

"How's Jessica taking all this?" Todd asked. He and Elizabeth were kneeling side by side on the basement floor, working on their separate signs. Jessica and Elizabeth didn't travel in the same circles, but Jessica normally would have stopped in to say hello and grab a slice of pizza. Todd had clearly noticed her conspicuous absence, as had everyone else in the group.

Elizabeth sighed. She didn't look up from the letters she was painting in yellow tempera. "Not well, as you can imagine. We're one hundred and eighty degrees apart on this."

Todd curved a finger under Elizabeth's chin and grinned when she looked at him. "So what's different about that?" he teased.

Elizabeth felt better, and she returned his smile. "Not much, I guess." She shrugged, and her expression was serious again. "It's just that . . . well . . . I wish Jess and I could agree on something for once."

Todd chuckled. "You don't want much, do you, Liz?"

"No," Elizabeth laughed, adding a flower to Todd's sign with a few squiggles of yellow paint. "Not much."

Elizabeth was up early the next morning. Dressed in jeans, a T-shirt, and sneakers, her sun-streaked blond hair wound neatly into a French braid, she was loading protest signs into the small back space of the Fiat when her father came out of the house to pick the newspaper up off the step.

He walked across the lawn, read one of the signs, and grinned. "Reminds me of the sixties," he said. "We had sit-ins, sing-ins, and sleep-ins."

Elizabeth laughed, though her mood was a little on the dark side. "This is a walk-in," she told her dad, pulling the Fiat keys from the pocket of her jeans. "We're going to march in front of the courthouse. Democracy in action."

"Good luck," Mr. Wakefield said as he scanned the front page of the paper.

"Dad?"

Mr. Wakefield gave his daughter a friendly, questioning look.

She sighed. "Jess is really furious with me."

"I suppose she is," Mr. Wakefield agreed. "You two are certainly poles apart on this issue."

"What about you, Dad?" Elizabeth pressed. "Where do you stand on beauty pageants?"

Mr. Wakefield smiled. "Squarely on neutral ground," he answered. "You and your sister are going to have to work this one out on your own."

# Four

Jessica was waiting on Monday morning when the principal's secretary pinned the list of Sweet Valley High pageant entrants to the bulletin board outside the office. Her own name was there, along with Amy's. Half a dozen sophomores had signed up—no competition so far—but two other people listed worried Jessica. Just a little.

Maggie Simmons, for one. A junior, Maggie was a talented actress who had attended a special theatrical high school in L.A. and starred in a number of plays there before her family's move to Sweet Valley. According to rumor, Maggie had even had a few bit parts in the movies. She was a pretty redhead with big green eyes.

The second bothersome name was Sharon Jefferson. Sharon was a senior, an excellent student liked by both teachers and kids. Sharon wasn't beautiful, but she was very attractive and she'd consistently won a place on the honor roll. Despite a serious hearing impairment, she played classical piano. What if the judges voted for her because she had not let her handicap inhibit her?

Jessica sighed. No one at Sweet Valley High, except for Elizabeth, of course, could compare to her when it came to looks. But Jessica hadn't even considered the possibility that someone might outshine her in the talent segment of the pageant.

Jessica was nibbling at her lower lip, deep in thought, when Amy came up beside her. She scanned the names on the typewritten list, then turned to look at Jessica with a blend of shock, betrayal, and anger in her eyes.

"I should have known!" she hissed.

Amy's fury didn't faze Jessica in the least. If there was one thing she thrived on, it was competition. At least, competition with someone like Amy. Maggie and Sharon could be another matter entirely.

"Known what?" Jessica asked innocently.

"That you *definitely* planned to enter the Miss Teen Sweet Valley pageant!"

Jessica smiled and started off toward her

locker. Amy came along, still visibly annoyed. "It took me a while to make up my mind," Jessica said.

"Now I'll have some real competition," Amy fretted.

Jessica smiled sweetly at her friend and tried to seem modest. "Don't be silly, Amy. You have as much chance to win as anybody."

Although Amy still seemed upset, she relaxed a little with Jessica's praise. Jessica had learned a long time ago that she could get Amy to settle down by flattering her.

Amy sighed. "I guess you're right," she said.

And then Amy dropped her bomb. "I heard the winner is going to be awarded *ten* thousand dollars," she said, her voice hushed with awe.

Jessica stopped dead in the busy hallway and stared at her friend. She was sure she remembered Lila saying the prize was only five thousand. *"Ten thousand dollars?"* she echoed, and the words squeaked a little because her throat had gone tight. "You're kidding!"

Amy shook her head wisely. "It's true, Jess. I overheard some kids talking about it at the beach on Saturday."

If it wasn't for Maggie's acting ability and Sharon's talent at the piano, Jessica would have been walking about a foot off the floor from sheer delight. With that much money she could get an even better car. And Jessica intended to be generous. She would let Elizabeth drive it once in a while.

Probably.

"What are you doing for the talent competition?" Amy asked as she and Jessica reached their lockers.

Jessica was still feeling secretive, and a bit worried, about her plans to dance, particularly since she had seen Maggie's and Sharon's names on the pageant contestant list. She just shrugged. "I haven't decided," she lied. "Are you still going to do a baton routine?"

Amy got out her math book and closed her locker door. She frowned a bit as she nodded.

Jessica hid a smile.

By the time lunch rolled around, Jessica had managed to quiet all her fears. OK, so there was more to winning a beauty pageant than being good-looking. She had always known that, even if Elizabeth pretended not to. Both Sharon and Maggie were talented, popular, and smart. But so was Jessica, after all. Everyone had always said she was a born dancer, and that with a little training she could be a professional.

Elizabeth's voice rose softly over the general clatter of the cafeteria as Jessica carried her tray toward the table where Amy and Lila were already waiting for her.

"Hi, Jess."

Jessica's nod was cool. She couldn't forget that her sister was actively campaigning to ruin the Miss Teen Sweet Valley contest. Elizabeth had gathered signatures all over town and talked to practically every student and teacher at Sweet Valley High. While Jessica had been sleeping in on Saturday morning, Elizabeth had been leading a protest march at City Hall. If Jessica didn't miss her guess, there would be a blistering article with Elizabeth's byline in the next edition of *The Oracle*.

"Hello, Liz," Jessica answered, barely pausing.

Elizabeth started to say something, stopped, and then said, "Feel free to use the Fiat if you want to. Todd is taking me home."

"Great," Jessica said, without the touch of friendliness or enthusiasm she would have added at another time. She took the set of car keys Elizabeth held out to her, nodded her thanks, and walked away.

Elizabeth sighed as she watched her sister sit down with Amy and Lila and some of the others in her crowd.

"This division over the beauty pageant is starting to get to you, isn't it, Liz?" Enid asked. She wasn't Elizabeth's best friend for nothing: the two girls had a lot in common, and at times they could almost read each other's minds.

"It's not like it's anything new," Elizabeth answered. "But it certainly isn't going to help matters any when the new issue of *The Oracle* comes out tomorrow."

Todd shrugged, though his expression was gentle and sympathetic. "What's the big deal? You and Jessica have had differences of opinion lots of times, and neither of you has disowned the other yet."

Elizabeth shrugged as she thought of the way she had roundly denounced both beauty pageants and the people who entered them in her piece for the school newspaper. Her opinions hadn't changed since she'd written the article, but still, she never liked having a strain between herself and Jessica.

"Look at it this way," Enid said, opening her milk carton and sticking a straw inside. "Whether we succeed in getting the pageant canceled or not, the whole controversy will be ancient history in a couple of weeks."

Elizabeth shook her head sadly. "I wish it were that simple," she said. "If we don't stop this sexist exhibition, there will be another one just like it next year. And the year after that."

Todd grinned at her. "Hey, cheer up, will you? This isn't brain surgery, Liz. We're not talking life or death."

Elizabeth and Enid laughed. "You have a

way of putting things into perspective, you know that, Wilkins?'' Elizabeth said.

Piano music flowed through the open doors of the auditorium at Sweet Valley High. It seemed to sparkle and dance in the air around Jessica as she stood listening after school that day.

"This is not a favorable development," she murmured to herself as she stepped into the shadows at the back of the enormous room.

Sharon Jefferson was seated at the baby grand piano on one side of the stage. Her hands flowed gracefully over the keys, and her concentration was so intense that Jessica could feel it.

Jessica thought of the flashy silver convertible she meant to buy with the prize money from the pageant, as well as the clothes and jewelry she would bring home from the shopping spree. Doubts began to creep into her mind, but she pushed them firmly aside, more determined than ever to win the title.

No one—*no one*—was more qualified to reign as Miss Teen Sweet Valley than she was.

Resolutely, Jessica turned and walked out of the auditorium.

The faithful Fiat was waiting when Jessica reached the school parking lot. She slipped behind the wheel, started the engine, and headed for home.

By the time Mrs. Wakefield got home from work, Jessica had cleaned her room, done a load of laundry, and put a simple casserole into the oven to cook. She was hacking vegetables into salad-sized pieces when her mother entered the kitchen and gave her daughter a tired smile.

"Well, Jess, hi. This is a surprise."

Jessica shrugged, her hair brushing her cheek as she bent to peer into the oven at the simmering food. "It was my turn to fix dinner," she said.

Mrs. Wakefield smiled and pushed a tendril of blond hair back from her face. She was a beautiful woman, an older version of Jessica and Elizabeth. "I see," she said in an amused tone as she set down her briefcase. "Is Elizabeth home?"

"Don't know," Jessica answered without looking at her mother. This was no time to discuss her grievances with her twin, important as they were.

Mrs. Wakefield took a cup from the cabinet and an herbal-tea bag from a canister. After adding water to the cup, she set it in the microwave to heat. "Things have been pretty tense between you and Elizabeth lately," she said casually.

Jessica felt her shoulders stiffen slightly, but she still tried to maintain her unruffled attitude. "Sometimes Liz can be pretty unreasonable," she remarked. Though her voice was even, her temper was seething and bubbling like the casserole in the oven.

The bell on the microwave chimed and Mrs. Wakefield took out her tea. She dropped the tea bag into the trash and sat down at the kitchen table before replying. "Elizabeth feels very strongly about the beauty pageant," she said moderately.

Jessica put the finished salad into the refrigerator and began to clean up the mess on the counter. "So do I," she answered, miffed. "This is a terrific chance for me to do something really important, and if Liz gets her way, she'll wreck it for me."

"I don't think her campaign to have the pageant canceled should be seen as a personal attack against you," Mrs. Wakefield said. "Your father and I are doing our best to stay out of this, but I admit I'm concerned about the hostility between you two."

Jessica stuffed peelings and stems into the garbage disposal and then took some satisfaction in grinding them up. She washed and dried her hands before turning to meet her mother's gaze. "How do you and Dad feel about this?" she asked. "Are you going to stay home on pageant night, if there is one, or will you be there to cheer me on?''

Mrs. Wakefield rose from her chair to give Jessica a brief but reassuring hug. "Of course we'll be there. What gave you the idea we wouldn't?"

Jessica was surprised to discover how relieved she was. "I guess I thought you'd agree with Elizabeth."

Mrs. Wakefield smiled. "Whatever our private opinions might be, Jessica, you're our daughter. Your father and I love you very much."

Jessica smiled. It was good to hear her mother talk like that. Now the Wakefields were a tight family unit again, but not so long ago tensions between Mr. and Mrs. Wakefield had become almost unbearable and Mr. Wakefield had moved out of the house. For a while, at least, Jessica, Elizabeth, and Steven had all thought their parents might end up getting a divorce.

"Thanks," Jessica said. She checked the casserole and then got out dishes and silverware to set the table while her mother relaxed and drank her tea. When she sensed the moment was right, Jessica leaned back against the counter, folded her arms, and smiled. "There *is* one thing I wanted to talk to you about."

Mrs. Wakefield had finished her tea, and she looked relaxed. "What's that, sweetheart?"

Jessica ran the tip of her tongue over her dry lips. "Well, it's about the talent portion of the contest," she ventured. "I plan to dance, but—well, let's face it, I'm a little rusty. And I'm up against some pretty heavy-duty competition."

Mrs. Wakefield arched one perfectly shaped eyebrow, and Jessica thought she saw her mother's lips twitch with amusement. It was clear she was beginning to get a glimmer that her daughter might have a reason for being so eager to help with dinner. "Go on."

"The point is," Jessica rushed on eagerly, "I think I need some lessons to sort of brush up."

"That's a good idea," Mrs. Wakefield said, but her tone of voice and her expression were strictly noncommittal.

Jessica gave a theatrical sigh. "The problem is, I spent the last of my allowance on the music and the leotard and tights for my dance number."

"Ah," said Mrs. Wakefield. "You're broke."

Jessica spread her hands in a gesture of help-less consternation, as if someone else had spent her allowance for her. "Flat," she said, blowing so that her bangs danced against her forehead.

It seemed that Mrs. Wakefield could not be prompted into doing what Jessica wanted. She was going to make her daughter ask.

"I need to borrow money to pay for a crash course in modern dance," Jessica finally blurted out. "I've already called the best studio in town, and they have an opening, but I'll have to act fast."

"What are your terms, Jessica?"

Jessica raised both eyebrows, puzzled. "Terms?"

"Yes. How do you intend to pay me back?"

A dazzling smile broke over Jessica's face. "You mean you're going to lend me the money?"

Mrs. Wakefield smiled again. "Provided we can come to some satisfactory agreement, yes. This isn't a gift, after all; it's a loan."

With dance lessons, Jessica would surely win the contest, and that meant she would have ten thousand dollars to spend. She wasn't worried about paying back the small amount she needed to borrow. It would be easy. "OK. We'll work something out."

"Not something," Mrs. Wakefield said, her manner pleasant but firm. "I'll be deducting fifty percent of your allowance until the full amount is paid off."

Jessica nodded quickly, ready to agree to anything that would cinch the Miss Teen Sweet Valley pageant for her. "Thanks, Mom," she said.

Mrs. Wakefield took her checkbook and a pen from her briefcase. "How much?" she asked.

Jessica told her mother the amount the dance studio secretary had mentioned when she had

51

called for information. Mrs. Wakefield wrote the check and handed it to her daughter.

"Remember, Jess," she cautioned. "Debts always have to be paid, one way or another."

It was all Jessica could do not to dance around the kitchen in sheer joy. She would think about debts later; right then all she cared about was wowing the judges on pageant night and coming home with that crown glittering on her head—and the key to Frazer's heart in her hand.

When she joined her family at the table, however, and came face-to-face with Elizabeth, some of Jessica's optimism and excitement faded. Mr. and Mrs. Wakefield would be in the audience on pageant night to see Jessica win all that money and all those prizes, their faces filled with pride in their daughter's accomplishments.

Providing Elizabeth didn't manage to ruin everything first.

# Five

Jessica had just finished reading Elizabeth's article in *The Oracle* when she caught a ride with Lila to Krezenski's Dance Studio the next afternoon. Her ego was stinging from the things Elizabeth had said about beauty pageants and the people who participated in them. Even now, snatches of the article ran through her mind. . . .

*Contests like this set the cause of women's rights back generations. . . . Women who enter and support them are, for all practical intents and purposes, betraying their own sex. . . .*

Lila raised both eyebrows when she brought the car to a stop in front of the studio. It was located in an old, seedy-looking building with brick arches over the windows.

"You'd think a famous teacher like Mr. Krezenski could afford a better studio," she commented.

Jessica wasn't interested in Lila's opinion of the neighborhood. "I'll see you later," she said, jumping out of Lila's expensive car and reaching into the back seat for her purse. She'd put her textbooks in the Fiat earlier so that Elizabeth could take them home. "Thanks for the ride, and remember to keep this a secret."

Lila gave the aging building another disapproving look, shuddered, then shrugged. "Sure. See you tomorrow."

Jessica hurried into the studio, filled out a brief form, and gave the receptionist the check her mother had written the night before. After that she was directed to the dressing room, where she was supposed to change her clothes.

Because she was saving her white leotard and tights for the pageant, Jessica wore a pale blue exercise outfit she'd borrowed from Elizabeth— without consulting her sister, of course. The big mirror covering the opposite wall told her she looked terrific.

Six other girls, of different ages but all slender and graceful, were stretching at the bar while scratchy music played in a corner of the room. A man with snow-white hair and piercing blue eyes approached Jessica. His face wore a thoughtful expression.

"You are a new student?" he asked, speaking with a heavy Eastern European accent.

Jessica's confidence wavered a little under the man's stern and serious gaze. "Well, sort of," she said nervously. "I've never attended your classes before, but I have had several years of dance."

Mr. Krezenski nodded, but he still didn't smile. When he suddenly clapped his hands together in a series of sharp slaps, Jessica jumped.

"Let us be started," the dance instructor called out in his funny, awkward English, and all the girls scurried to the center of the room to stand in a straight line.

Jessica took a place at one end, nervously tugging the back of her blue leotard into place. Until that day, she had known Mr. Krezenski only by reputation. Elizabeth had watched a special on public television about his career as a dancer and his dramatic, daring escape from some little country in Eastern Europe, and she had talked about practically nothing else for a week after the show. Jessica had pictured the man as young, handsome, and very romantic, and now she was disappointed.

About half an hour of the class had passed when Jessica's troubles really began.

"No, no, *no!*" Mr. Krezenski yelled suddenly, clapping his hands again and then stopping the music by grabbing the arm of the ancient phonograph and wrenching the needle off the record. Obviously, the man liked to do everything the old-fashioned way.

He came to stand in front of Jessica, his hands resting on his hips, and glared into her face. "Do not fling yourself from side to side as if you expected to fly away like Peter Pan!"

Angry, embarrassed color flooded Jessica's cheeks. She was about to turn and walk out when she remembered how well Sharon Jefferson played the piano. And rumor had it that Maggie Simmons was going to perform a dramatic scene from Shakespeare at the pageant. If Jessica wanted to win the title of Miss Teen Sweet Valley, and she definitely did, she was going to have to stick this out. Besides, she had noticed a sign behind the reception desk that said NO REFUNDS, and she didn't exactly want to go home and tell her mother she had wasted all that money by giving up her lessons on the very first day!

"Again!" shouted Mr. Krezenski. Without waiting for Jessica to comment, he stormed over to the dusty phonograph and set the needle back on the record.

Without looking at any of the other girls, Jessica bit her lower lip and began to dance.

She got through about four steps before Mr. Krezenski decided to humiliate her again.

"Stop, stop, stop!" he cried.

Jessica figured the mean guys in that faraway government of his had probably been glad to see Mr. Krezenski go. He was crabby in a major way. She let out her breath and her bangs bounced against her forehead. "What am I doing wrong now?"

Mr. Krezenski looked surprised at her question, and some of the others giggled. *Everything!* he bellowed. "You have the grace of a drunken moose, my dear! You dance as though you were wearing boots of lead!"

Tears stung in Jessica's eyes, but she was too proud to cry in front of the man or his students. She lifted her chin and held her shoulders very straight.

"Watch Marlena," the instructor barked, pointing toward the tall, willowy girl standing next to Jessica. "Dance as she does, like the gazelle!"

Jessica would have bet six months' allowance that things couldn't get worse. If she had, she'd have lost, because Mr. Krezenski didn't give her a moment's peace from then until the class ended.

After the lesson, Jessica was hiding out in the dressing room, drying her sweaty face with a towel, when she looked up and saw Marlena standing beside her. Suddenly Jessica remembered seeing the dancer in the halls at Sweet Valley High.

"You're Jessica Wakefield, aren't you?"

Jessica's spirits rose a little. Finally, someone who understood that she was popular and important and should be treated with respect! She nodded and smiled.

"Elizabeth's sister," Marlena said with admiration. "I really wish I could write the way she does. That article she wrote about beauty pageants was really hard-hitting."

"Hard-hitting" was a good description, Jessica thought ruefully. When she had read Elizabeth's article she'd felt as if someone had hit *her*. Hard.

"Right," Jessica said. She put on her shorts and tank top and left the studio. To her relief, Mrs. Wakefield was waiting in her car.

"How did it go?" she asked as Jessica flung herself into the seat with a heavy sigh and fastened the seat belt.

Jessica tilted her head back and closed her eyes. At that moment the only thing she wanted more than a shower and a dip in the pool was the Miss Teen Sweet Valley title. And that seemed as if it might be a lot harder to get than she'd ever imagined it could be. "It was a nightmare," she breathed. "The man hates me."

Mrs. Wakefield chuckled. "So the lessons are harder than you expected, huh?"

"They are *hideous*," Jessica raved, flinging her

hands wide. "Mr. Krezenski is a monster, and he's not going to be satisfied until he's stomped my ego right into the floor!"

Her mother smiled as she pulled out into the light traffic. "Honestly, Jess, was it really that bad?"

"I'm not planning to quit, if that's what you're asking," Jessica muttered as she covered her eyes with her hand. "But I sure feel like it."

"We can't always do what we feel like doing," Mrs. Wakefield pointed out with quiet good humor.

"Don't I know it?" Jessica moaned. She turned and looked at her mother earnestly. "Just don't tell anyone I'm taking lessons, OK? If I do fall on my face, I don't want everybody in the world to be in on the joke."

"I've already mentioned it to your father. After all, it's his money, too, that's paying for the lessons," Mrs. Wakefield said. "But I won't say anything to Steven or Elizabeth if you don't want me to."

"Good. Let's keep it our secret."

Minutes later they were home. Jessica headed straight for the bathroom she shared with Elizabeth. Her head was throbbing. She gulped down two aspirins, stripped off her clothes, and got into the shower.

After drying off, she put on a swimsuit. She

was already feeling much better now that she'd washed away the sweat and strain of her dance lesson, but a few minutes in the pool would help her unwind.

"Hi," Elizabeth said as Jessica passed through the kitchen, bare-footed and with a towel rolled up under one arm.

Jessica thought of all the misery she'd suffered during Mr. Krezenski's dance class, and how it would be all for nothing if Elizabeth had her way. Then she remembered the article Elizabeth had written for *The Oracle*. "Hello," she said in an icy tone. "That write-up in the school paper was a real hatchet job. Maybe we ought to call you Lizzie Borden from now on."

For a second Elizabeth looked hurt, but then she narrowed her eyes and said, "I was only expressing my opinion."

"Great," Jessica responded. "Just remember that *I* have the same right." She left the room, closing the door briskly behind her.

Later, at the dinner table, Steven reached for the mashed potatoes and dropped a spoonful onto his plate. Much to Jessica's disappointment, he hadn't brought Frazer McConnell home to dinner with him. "Lately, this place has all the charm and grace of Beirut," Steven said.

Jessica and Elizabeth were watching each other eat in cold silence.

Mr. Wakefield took a sip from his water glass and looked at his daughters thoughtfully. "I assume you're still battling it out over the beauty pageant," he asked presently.

Elizabeth's cheeks went pink. She gave Jessica a look flickering with blue fire before answering. "I have certain principles to uphold," she said coolly, "both as a woman and as a journalist."

Jessica leaned forward in her chair. She was totally steamed. "And I *don't* have principles, I suppose?" she shot back.

"Enough," Mr. Wakefield broke in. His voice was quiet but firm, and both twins knew he meant what he said. "Steven is right: this house is beginning to feel like a war zone." He gazed solemnly at Elizabeth and then at Jessica. "I want the two of you to sit down and talk this over in a spirit of compromise."

Elizabeth opened her mouth to say something, then closed it again.

Jessica was wary. "What kind of compromise?" she asked. Maybe she sounded as if she was offering an olive branch, but nothing short of an act of Congress would make her do what Elizabeth wanted her to do—quit the pageant.

"You could agree to disagree, for one thing," Mrs. Wakefield said.

61

"There is absolutely no question that we disagree," Elizabeth said stiffly.

Steven shook his head. "Why do I feel as if somebody just tossed a live grenade under the table?"

"Please excuse me," Jessica said with mock politeness. She pushed back her chair and glowered at Elizabeth. "I seem to have lost my appetite. Again."

"So have I," said Elizabeth, flinging down her napkin.

Mr. Wakefield looked at his wife and sighed. "I tried," he said.

"I know, dear," Mrs. Wakefield answered sympathetically.


The telephone rang early the next morning. Mr. and Mrs. Wakefield had both left for work, Steven had gone to his first class, and Jessica had barricaded herself in the bathroom. Elizabeth picked up the receiver of the hall phone.

"Wakefield residence," she said.

"May I please speak to Elizabeth Wakefield?" a female voice asked. "This is Angela Stone calling. I'm a reporter for the *Sweet Valley News*."

Elizabeth's heart leapfrogged right over one beat into another. "Hello, Ms. Stone," she said, and then introduced herself.

"Call me Angela," the reporter urged her. "Listen, Elizabeth, I read your article in *The Oracle* on the Chamber of Commerce's beauty pageant. You see, my daughter goes to Sweet Valley High, so I have the opportunity to read the school paper. I must say I was very impressed. We'd like to run the piece in our paper, if that's all right with you."

Elizabeth swallowed hard. All right? It was wonderful! "That would be fine," she said evenly.

"Good," Angela replied. "We'll print it in the evening edition. Congratulations on a well-written, concise piece of work, Elizabeth."

"Thank you," Elizabeth said, still feeling a little dazed.

Jessica opened the door to the bathroom and peeked around its edge. Her hair was wrapped in a towel and steam billowed around her like a cloud. "Who was that?" she asked. From the tone of her voice, anybody would have thought Elizabeth was a stranger.

Because she was eager to share the exciting news with someone, Elizabeth spoke as though she and Jessica hadn't been on the outs for days on end. "It was Angela Stone from the *Sweet Valley News*. They liked my article on beauty pageants, and they want to reprint it." A second after the words were out of her mouth, Elizabeth wished she could call them back.

Jessica's expression was decidedly un-friendly. "Oh, great. Now the whole commu-nity is going to be treated to that—that *sermon* of yours!" Jessica disappeared into the bath-room and slammed the door.

Elizabeth sighed and walked back to her bed-room. "Oh, well," she said to the reflection in her mirror. "Having a sister was great while it lasted."

It was a relief when, a little while later, Todd came to pick her up for school. Elizabeth wasn't up to another round with Jessica. "The *Sweet Valley News* is going to reprint my article!" she told her boyfriend excitedly as he backed his BMW out of the Wakefields' driveway.

Todd grinned, obviously impressed. "Wow, Liz, that's great."

She sighed. "I'm afraid the news didn't win me any points with Jessica," she confessed.

Todd squeezed her hand. "Look, Liz, if this is bothering you so much, maybe you should just back off and stop fighting this pagent thing. Let Enid and the others spearhead the project. That would make things all right be-tween you and Jess again."

Elizabeth badly wanted to be on good terms with her sister once more, but she couldn't just abandon her principles. "I really believe that beauty pageants are demeaning and destructive, Todd," she said sadly. "I can't pretend otherwise, even for Jessica."

They stopped at a light and he leaned over to kiss her lightly. "Don't take all this too seriously, Liz," he added. "Like I said before, the beauty pageant is not exactly a matter of life and death."

Maybe it wasn't, but sometimes it felt like one to Elizabeth. She loved her sister, and now a wall had been built between them, one that might be very hard to tear down.

"If I could just make her understand," she whispered.

Todd started the car again. "I have a feeling Jessica is thinking the same thing about you," he remarked.

Elizabeth punched him playfully in the shoulder. "I hate it when you make so much sense," she laughed. Right then she made up her mind to find Jessica after school. The two of them would talk until they'd worked through the problem and things were back to normal, whether Jessica liked it or not.

# Six

Elizabeth watched as her sister read the article in the *Sweet Valley News*, and she braced herself for the inevitable explosion.

Instead of blowing up, however, Jessica just tossed the folded newspaper aside and headed for her room without a word to Elizabeth or a glance in her direction. Only the stiffness in the set of Jessica's slender shoulders gave away her annoyance.

Once again, dinner was a strained affair, and when the telephone rang during dessert, Mr. Wakefield looked relieved to answer it.

When he returned to the dining room, he seemed both amused and bewildered. "The local TV station would like to interview the both of you," he said, looking from Jessica to

Elizabeth. "It seems they were intrigued by the reprint of Elizabeth's article in the *Sweet Valley News*, and they noticed your name on the list of entrants, Jessica. They want to do a piece on the evening news, something about sisters being on opposing sides of the same issue."

Elizabeth was both nervous and excited. Appearing on a local channel would give her a valuable forum for discussing her views. Seeing the smug little smile on Jessica's face, she knew her sister was thinking the same thing. Thanks to the wonders of modern technology, the girls would now be able to debate the subject on a much wider scale!

"What did you tell them?" Jessica inquired.

Mr. Wakefield picked up his spoon and reached for his half-eaten pudding. "That the decision would be up to my daughters. I wrote the woman's name and number on the note pad beside the phone."

Jessica and Elizabeth both excused themselves hastily and raced to the telephone.

Elizabeth got there first. "Well?" she asked, lifting the receiver. "What's the word, Jess? Yes or no? Do we hold the Great Debate or not?"

Jessica folded her suntanned arms. She sincerely believed in what she said next. "Yes, of course. I want the chance to let the world know what's *right* about beauty pageants, such as how they bring out the best in people and provide opportunities the contestants might not have had otherwise. I think they can make a real difference in people's lives. And they're *not* just for airheads!"

Elizabeth made the call.

Jessica had butterflies in her stomach when the TV crew arrived at Sweet Valley High the next morning during second-period study hall. This was her opportunity to undo some of the damage Elizabeth had done with her article, the picket, and the petition-signing campaign. Jessica loved the idea of being on TV, but she was nervous. After all, there was a lot at stake. Her convictions were just as strong as Elizabeth's, and it was up to her to clear up this crazy idea that beauty pageants were destructive.

She and Elizabeth sat side by side in the cafeteria, which was empty except for the twins, the TV people, and the kitchen workers. By accident rather than by design, the girls had worn their hair in a similar style, a simple French braid.

"You're mirror images of each other," the reporter commented with a grin. He was handsome, probably just a few years out of college—the kind of guy Jessica hoped to attract once she'd won her title.

Elizabeth seemed relaxed, which irritated Jessica.

"We look alike, of course," Elizabeth said politely. "But personality-wise, we're very different."

"So I hear," the reporter said as he scanned the notes in his hand. The crew was setting up lights and finding the right camera angles. "Elizabeth?" He raised his eyes and looked inquiringly at both girls, and Elizabeth lifted one index finger to identify herself.

Jessica shifted uncomfortably in her chair.

The lights flared to life and the camera began to whir, and the TV reporter introduced himself to the audience. Then he presented Elizabeth and Jessica as identical twins who attended Sweet Valley High and found themselves on opposite sides of a very hot local issue.

"Elizabeth," he said, "you wrote an article for *The Oracle*, your school paper, in which you said that beauty pageants were insulting to women. The piece was subsequently picked up by the *Sweet Valley News*."

Elizabeth nodded, acting as cool and calm as if she were on TV every day of the week.

"And Jessica," the reporter went on, turning his bright smile on her. In his own way, he was every bit as good-looking as Frazer, Jessica thought. "Ironically, you're a contestant in the very pageant your sister is denouncing. How do you feel about her views?"

Jessica made a point to smile sweetly. After all, the pageant judges would probably be watching, and she wanted to stand out in their minds. "I think she's wrong, of course. Beauty pageants bring out the best in people." She thought of her dance lessons with Mr. Krezenski. "They're hard work, too. In fact, I'd go so far as to say that a beauty pageant can make the difference between being a nobody and being a somebody."

Elizabeth waited for her turn. "Actually, beauty contests are outdated. I would like to believe we've grown beyond them. After all, what virtue is there in parading around on stage in a swimsuit and high heels?" She paused for a breath while Jessica seethed behind a serene expression. "Millions of little girls watch the national pageants," she went on a beat later, "and they form what I consider to be some very harmful attitudes about personal value."

The reporter held out his microphone to Jessica again, and this time she felt a wave of panic wash over her. Elizabeth had sounded so *sensible*. "Someone will win some very nice prizes," she blurted out, and after that the interview was a blur to Jessica. She just kept vaguely arguing that pageants gave young women a way to make something of themselves.

Elizabeth's statements kept intruding on Jessica's thoughts. In her mind's eye she saw the "millions of little girls" Elizabeth had mentioned, staring blindly at their television sets and thinking they had to look like Miss America to be considered important.

Jessica managed to shake off the disturbing picture as she got into the Fiat after school. She truly believed that intelligence, poise, and talent counted in pageants, too, and no one was going to convince her otherwise. Why, pageant winners had gone on to become community leaders and high-powered professionals. Some became famous newswomen, and some, popular television actresses. Who knew what was in store for her?

When Jessica arrived at the studio for dance class, only Marlena and Mr. Krezenski were there. The others were having their lesson in another room, the instructor explained, with an assistant.

With only Marlena in the room with her, Jessica felt more conspicuous than ever. But at the same time she was relieved to know the rest of the class wouldn't be around to smirk and giggle at her.

"Let us get started!" Mr. Krezenski barked with the usual sharp clap of his hands. Then he walked over to the record player and started the music.

For about ten minutes, Jessica danced as gracefully as she could to the scratchy music, but she still could not please Mr. Krezenski.

He spoke gruffly to her and made her stand by the bar and watch while Marlena executed the steps he wanted to see. When Marlena had finished he congratulated her on her hard work and talent, and his wrinkled face crinkled into a warm smile.

Jessica longed to earn the same kind of praise, and when Mr. Krezenski motioned for her to resume the dance, she put all her heart and soul into the movement. But when the class was finally over Mr. Krezenski only shook his bushy white head in obvious disgust and walked away from Jessica.

It took all of Jessica's determination not to burst into tears of anger and hurt. She was Jessica Wakefield, one of the prettiest and most popular girls at Sweet Valley High. She was co-captain of the cheerleading squad and, while her grades weren't quite on par with Elizabeth's, she was bright. Who did this man think he was, treating her like an untalented, lazy idiot?

Her motions were brisk and furious as she

stripped off her dance clothes, stuffed them into her bag, and pulled on white shorts and a bright yellow top. Marlena had already left, this time without trying to strike up any kind of conversation with her fellow student, and Jessica was bothered by that, too. A girl could develop an inferiority complex hanging around this place.

Jessica was already out on the sidewalk when she brought herself up short, turned on her heel, and marched back into the old building. She found Mr. Krezenski in the studio, standing at the bar with his eyes closed, listening to his scratchy music.

His mouth curved into a small smile, as though he might be imagining that he could dance again.

Jessica cleared her throat. "Excuse me," she said, firmly but politely.

Mr. Krezenski opened his eyes wide, evidently surprised at Jessica's presence, and quickly turned off the record player. "Miss Wakefield," he said.

After drawing a deep breath for courage, Jessica walked over to stand directly facing her teacher. "There's something I want to ask you," she announced. Her voice trembled a little.

"Yes?" Mr. Krezenski prompted, gesturing somewhat impatiently with one hand. Jessica noticed that his fingers were wrinkled and slightly twisted.

"I think you're being very unfair to me," she burst out. "And I'd like to know why."

Mr. Krezenski waved toward two of the metal folding chairs that were against the opposite wall. "Let us sit down and discuss this question, Miss Wakefield," he said.

They took seats side by side, and Jessica knotted her fingers together in her lap.

"Everyone has always told me I have a lot of talent as a dancer," Jessica said boldly. "But you treat me as if I'm a fool, a complete beginner."

Jessica thought she saw a spark of humor flicker in the depths of Mr. Krezenski's eyes. "So, you think I am too hard on you, that I should not make you strive to do your best work?"

Jessica was confused; she hadn't thought about the situation from that particular angle. "It's just that you're—well, *mean*," she finally said.

The smile in Mr. Krezenski's eyes spread to his mouth. "Yes, Miss Wakefield," he admitted, "I am a mean man, if you like. Legions of my students would agree with you. But I am only hard on dancers who have talent and potential. The others, I have no time for. I send them on their way."

Jessica's heart did a little skip. "You mean, you *do* think I'm talented?"

"Very talented," said Mr. Krezenski. "But you are also stubborn, lazy, and not a little arrogant, Miss Wakefield. You do not put your whole being into the dancing. Instead, you are always preoccupied with some other matter."

Jessica sighed. All along she'd thought she was giving the dance lessons her best shot. Now she realized Mr. Krezenski was right. She'd been thinking about the pageant, the prizes, and the admiration she would see in Frazer McConnell's eyes once she had won the title.

Jessica ran the tip of her tongue over her lips. "I'll concentrate harder, I promise," she said.

Mr. Krezenski wagged an index finger at her. "And I promise," he told her with good-natured gruffness, "to be as difficult as ever. It is the only way I know to get the best from my dancers."

Jessica was exhausted from the class and the confrontation with the dance teacher, but she also felt an exhilarating excitement. Mr. Krezenski thought she was good, that she had potential. She could easily imagine herself soaring around the stage in the school auditorium, making the audience gasp at her grace and energy.

"Do you think I could take extra lessons, just

for the next week or so?'' she asked. Then she told Mr. Krezenski about the beauty pageant, and about how she planned to dance in the talent segment.

He smiled. ''I have read of this event in the newspaper,'' he said with a nod. ''Yes, Miss Wakefield, you may have extended class time. I would suggest you telephone your parents so that we can begin *this* evening.''

Although she'd been looking forward to going home, eating a big dinner, and crashing in her room, Jessica felt a new surge of energy. Knowing that Mr. Krezenski believed in her made a very big difference.

A little over an hour later, Jessica pulled into the driveway at home, sweaty and achy and full of renewed enthusiasm for the beauty pageant.

When she walked into the house, Elizabeth, Steven, and Mrs. Wakefield were in the family room watching the evening news. Evidently Mr. Wakefield was working late.

''The interview is on next,'' Mrs. Wakefield said eagerly as Jessica put down her dance bag and went to the kitchen for a cold drink and her dinner. The plate had been carefully wrapped, and Jessica put it into the microwave to heat. Then she returned and stood in the doorway of the family room to watch the TV.

She looked terrific on screen, if she did say

so herself, Jessica thought as she sipped her soda. But it was Elizabeth who came off as the smart, savvy teen-with-a-mission.

"You were both wonderful," Mrs. Wakefield said when the interview was over.

Elizabeth smiled, though there was something sad about her expression. Jessica shrugged and went to take her dinner out of the microwave. She was just sitting down at the kitchen table to eat when Steven came into the room. Mrs. Wakefield and Elizabeth followed.

"Your big scene has been saved for posterity, girls," he told his sisters as he held up a video tape in one hand. He set the recording down on the table and opened the refrigerator door to inspect the contents. "Isn't anybody going to ask me how it feels to be the brother of the famous, if controversial, Wakefield twins?"

"No," Jessica, Elizabeth, and Mrs. Wakefield all answered at the same time.

Steven shook his head and pretended to be bewildered. He took a piece of chicken from a platter in the fridge, and bit into it as he left the kitchen. Diplomatically, Mrs. Wakefield followed.

"Why did you get home so late, Jess? You almost missed the broadcast," Elizabeth said quietly.

Jessica shrugged. "I was busy."

"You looked great on TV," Elizabeth continued. She leaned against one of the counters and folded her arms.

"Thanks," Jessica replied, concentrating on her supper. She'd had a long day, and she wasn't up to another round with Elizabeth. "So did you," she added.

"How long are we going to keep this up?" Elizabeth asked, and this time her voice betrayed some frustration.

Jessica washed down a bite of chicken with a sip of her soda and lifted one shoulder in a bored shrug. "Keep what up?"

Elizabeth pulled out a chair and sat down at the table. "Come on, Jess, you *know* what I'm talking about. Things are getting pretty uncomfortable around here."

Jessica met her sister's gaze and lifted her chin a notch. "I guess you think the solution to that is for me to drop out of the pageant," she said. "Well, I'm not going to do that, Liz. I'm not only entering, I intend to win."

Elizabeth sighed and propped her chin in one hand. "I think Dad's right," she persisted. "You and I should talk this over. Maybe we could work out some kind of compromise."

"I'll tell you what kind of compromise I want, Liz," Jessica said briskly. She pushed back her chair and walked to the sink. After scraping the leftovers into the garbage disposal, she rinsed the plate and set it in the dishwasher along with her silverware. "I want **you** to get off my back about this pageant. **Furthermore**, it would be nice if you'd stop trying **to force** your opinions on everybody else."

Elizabeth's cheeks were pink, and she tightened her lips for a moment before replying, "I'm trying to be reasonable here, Jess. How about giving me a break?"

Jessica needed a shower, and she had some homework to do. This was not a good time to get her to compromise about anything. "Did you give me a break when you wrote that article, Liz? When you tried to make me look like a fool on TV? Is that your idea of being reasonable?" Jessica looked closely at her sister for a moment and then swept out of the kitchen and hurried to her room. Elizabeth was left alone to reflect on her sister's questions.

# Seven

"Well, look who decided to grace us with her presence," Amy Sutton said with an indignant toss of her head when Jessica sped into cheerleading practice in the gym the next afternoon.

Jessica ignored Amy, laid her books down on the bottom row of bleachers, and shook her hair back from her face. Then she took a deep breath and joined the other girls on the gym floor.

Practice lasted an hour, and when it was over Jessica rushed out of the gym with barely a wave for the rest of the squad.

At the dance studio, Jessica had a private lesson with Mr. Krezenski. She worked harder than she'd ever dreamed she could. And a strange thing happened. For the first time, she passed the point at which she wanted to collapse with exhaustion and found a new strength that carried her on.

"I saw you and your sister on the television news last night," Mr. Krezenski said when Jessica's lesson was over and she was drying her face with a towel.

Jessica was still struggling to get her breath. She braced herself for the inevitable criticism.

"The resemblance between the two of you is amazing," Mr. Krezenski went on in his peculiar, formal way. "But it is obvious that your opinions differ greatly."

Jessica knew Mr. Krezenski was going to take Elizabeth's side, and she felt her temper starting to flare. "You don't think I should enter the pageant?" she asked evenly.

Mr. Krezenski smiled. "My opinion does not matter, Miss Wakefield. It is my duty to instruct you in the dance; nothing less, nothing more."

Relieved, Jessica whispered a "thank you" and headed for the changing room.

"You, Jessica Wakefield, are getting to be a real bore," Lila Fowler observed, waving a french fry for emphasis. She and Jessica were sitting in the Dairi Burger that night, after having gone to a movie. "How long has it been since you've had a date, anyway?"

Jessica bristled. "Lots of guys have asked me out," she said stiffly. She and Lila were best friends, and they spent a lot of time together, but they were also very competitive. "I've just been really busy lately, that's all."

"You can say that again," Lila agreed. She gave Jessica a close, suspicious look. "You're taking this beauty pageant thing pretty seriously, aren't you?"

Jessica examined her glossy pink fingernails. "There comes a time in a girl's life," she answered without looking at Lila, "when she has to focus on a dream and give it everything she has."

Lila rolled her eyes, but didn't pursue the subject any further. As a general rule, she found other people's interests boring. "Here comes Amy and her boyfriend," she whispered.

Jessica smiled as Amy and Barry approached the table, holding hands. Since she had discovered that Jessica was a fellow contestant in the beauty pageant, Amy had been a little less friendly to Jessica, but not exactly cold. In fact, there was an attractive, warm glow about Amy lately that worried Jessica just a little. If that's what having a steady boyfriend did for a girl's complexion and attitude, Jessica thought grimly, maybe she should think about hooking one herself before the day of the pageant!

Lila invited the couple to sit down, and Barry

looked as if he wanted to accept. But Amy stopped him by grasping his arm. "We'll just sit over here," she said. Her smile was just a bit teasing as she wagged her fingers at Jessica. "Bye."

"Bye," Jessica answered lightly, making it clear that the encounter hadn't ruffled her.

Amy and Barry had just walked away when Elizabeth and Todd and a crowd of their friends came into the Dairi Burger. Elizabeth laughed happily at something Todd said. But when her eyes caught Jessica's, a strange sadness was evident.

Even though she was in a room full of noise and people, Jessica felt a momentary stab of loneliness. Still, she would not allow Elizabeth to see her in anything resembling a state of vulnerability. The way Elizabeth had been campaigning lately, who knew? She might use *anything* to her advantage.

Elizabeth stopped beside the table, her hands in the pockets of her neon pink windbreaker. "Hi, Jess," she said.

Jessica gave her sister a frosty little smile, "Hello," she answered in a voice that chimed with insincerity. "Taking time off from your selfless crusade to rid the world of beauty pageants?"

Elizabeth sighed and pulled her hands out of her pockets so that she could fold her arms.

"Yes," she replied. "Maybe you could take a break, too, Jess. From being so hostile!"

Lila was clearly pleased that the twins were on the outs. "Let's pull in our claws, Liz," she said. "No sense in making a public spectacle."

"You stay out of this!" Elizabeth said, her cheeks going pink with anger. But when she saw that Jessica had no intention of starting peace talks in the middle of the Dairi Burger, she sighed again and walked away.

Her friends followed, and Enid cast Jessica a puzzled look over one shoulder.

Lila giggled cattily. "Who would have thought Miss Supercool, Elizabeth Wakefield, would lose her temper like that?"

Jessica reached for her purse and stood. "Oh, shut up, Lila," she said. And then she paid for her fries and soda and left the Dairi Burger.

When Jessica reached home, she was met with both good news and bad news. The good news was that Frazer had come home with Steven. They were in the kitchen eating pizza.

The bad news was that Frazer had a girl with him: a tall, slender brunette with glistening hair that tumbled down her suntanned back, perfect coral fingernails, and a musical laugh. Cara Walker, Steven's girlfriend, introduced Frazer's date as her cousin Barbara. Barbara, it seemed, was a junior, like Jessica and Cara, though she went to high school in another town.

Jessica managed a stiff smile, turned down Steven's good-natured suggestion that she stay for a slice of pizza, spoke a few brief but friendly words to Cara, and headed for her room.

There, in the cluttered privacy of her own space, Jessica gave free rein to her frustration. She threw her purse in one direction and her sweater in the other. She kicked off her shoes one at a time and they flew across the room, each making a *ker-thunk* sound as it struck the closet door.

OK, Barbara was gorgeous, Jessica was willing to admit that. But she was no better-looking than Jessica, and she wasn't older, either. What did Frazer see in *her* that he didn't see in *Jessica*?

Jessica tried to put her brother's friend out of her mind, but all she could think about was his dark suntan, muscular build, and sun-bleached hair. Just holding the image of him in her mind made Jessica's heart thump.

And she might have been an empty pizza box, for all the attention he'd paid her in the kitchen a few minutes before!

Feeling very grumpy, Jessica showered, pulled a nightshirt over her head, and put her dance tape on to play. She'd read once that rehearsing mentally was almost as effective as the real thing. As she imagined herself performing her special routine and looking fabulous in her white leotard and tights, Jessica felt a little better.

A bit later on, she was sitting cross-legged on her bed, painting her toenails pink, when there was a knock at the door joining Jessica's room to the bathroom.

Jessica sighed. "Yo," she said.

Elizabeth came in. "I know I'm a glutton for punishment," she said with resignation, "but I'm here to try again. We really need to talk, Jess. Rationally."

Jessica frowned with concentration as she dabbed pearlescent liquid onto the nail of one big toe. "What is there to talk about, Liz?" she asked airily. "You certainly aren't willing to give any ground, and I'm not about to, either. That kind of leaves us with no subject, don't you think?"

Out of the corner of one eye Jessica could see Elizabeth leaning against the door to the bathroom, her hands behind her back. "Why is this so important to you?" she asked, and her voice sounded earnest. "Everybody at Sweet Valley High likes you. You're co-captain of the cheerleading squad, a member of Pi Beta Alpha, and a pretty good student—when you want to be! What could you possibly have to gain by being chosen Miss Teen Sweet Valley?"

Jessica thought first about mentioning the prizes involved in winning, then caught herself at the last moment. All she needed was for Elizabeth to get interested and decide to enter, too! That would be like having to compete with *herself*, and Jessica didn't need that kind of challenge. "I guess I just want to prove a point," she finally replied, resting her chin on one upraised knee as she continued to paint her toenails. She did not bother to look at Elizabeth. "Beauty pageants can be very positive experiences for everyone involved. I *could* end up with scholarships and maybe even modeling assignments and TV appearances. I might be the next big TV anchorwoman, for all you know. Besides, this is America, in case you've forgotten, and I have a right to make my own decisions. I don't need you hanging around like some censor, telling me what I should and shouldn't do."

"I haven't meant to be self-righteous," Elizabeth said, but to Jessica, her sister didn't sound the least bit apologetic. In fact, Jessica could sense Elizabeth's temper beginning to simmer behind that smooth, serene exterior. "It's just that I think these contests are harmful."

Jessica waved one hand in Elizabeth's direction and still didn't look at her. "Spare me the lecture, Liz," she said in a bored tone. "This is my big chance to make something of myself, maybe to get noticed for my talents, brains, *and* looks. I'm not going to blow it. And anyway, I've heard all your arguments before."

Elizabeth stepped closer to the bed, her hands on her hips. "You've heard them," she conceded, "but have you *listened?*"

"Yes!" Jessica snapped. She screwed the top back onto her polish and set the bottle down on her bedside table with a thump. "I've listened and listened and listened! And I'm just as bored as ever! I don't understand why you have to be so thick-headed and stubborn about this. You've got your writing. Is it so hard for you to understand that I have dreams, too?"

Elizabeth started to speak, stopped herself by biting her lower lip, then turned on her heel and left the room.

When Elizabeth had gone Jessica was surprised to realize that, instead of feeling triumphant, she wanted to cry. Being on the outs with her sister always made her feel as though a part of her was missing.

After Elizabeth had paced her room for a few minutes, waiting for her anger and frustration to subside, she got out her journal, found a pen, and stretched out on her bed to write. At first her feelings came in a flood, so fast and furious that she could hardly make sense of them. But as she wrote, she began to get a better perspective on the situation.

Maybe she would succeed at stopping the beauty pageant and maybe she would fail. Either way, she and Jessica would eventually get through this hard time and be friends again, as well as sisters.

At least, she hoped so.


"Do you think this is doing any good?" Enid asked uncertainly as she and Elizabeth stood in the Valley Mall the next afternoon, passing out flyers urging people to call the city councilors and protest the pageant.

Elizabeth's confidence was wavering a little. Although she still believed in what she was doing, she kept hearing Jessica's voice over and over again, accusing her of acting like a censor.

She made an effort to answer positively. "Of course," she answered finally. "It's doing a lot of good."

"I don't know," Enid said. "The last four people I've stopped have looked at me as if they thought I was a member of some weird religion."

Elizabeth laughed. "I guess that's the price we have to pay for standing up for what we believe in," she said. She formed the leftover flyers into a neat pile and then tucked them into her book bag. "Come on, let's go have a soda. We need a break."

They were passing Simple Splendor when Amy Sutton came out of the store carrying a big dress box. "Hello, Elizabeth," she said, a little distantly. "Hi, Enid. I just bought my dress for the pageant."

Elizabeth smiled. She knew Amy expected her to say something about the anti-pageant movement, but this was one time Amy was going to be disappointed. "That's nice," she said.

Amy indicated the dress box with a caressing motion of her fingers. "You might tell Jessica it's the prettiest, most expensive gown in the place," she went on, with a smug little grin.

Even though she wished Jessica had never *heard* of the Miss Teen Sweet Valley pageant, Elizabeth automatically defended her sister. "I don't think she'll be worried," she said sweetly.

Amy narrowed her eyes, said a brief goodbye, and stalked off.

Enid chuckled. "There's one thing you've got to admit, whatever your opinion of beauty pageants might be," she said, watching Amy go. "It takes raw courage to compete against Jessica Wakefield."

Elizabeth said nothing. The girls bought sodas, then sat down at a table on the concourse.

"Do you think Jessica will win?" Enid asked

after taking a sip of her drink. "Assuming we fail in our mission to save modern womanhood from the jaws of sexism, I mean?"

Although she was feeling a little blue, Elizabeth smiled at her friend's phrasing. "We're going to succeed," she assured Enid, though she wasn't completely convinced anymore.

"The pageant *is* next Saturday," Enid reminded her. "There are posters all over town, and I've even seen public-service announcements on TV."

"That's a laugh," Elizabeth said bitterly. "Since when does encouraging a bunch of women to walk around a stage half-naked constitute a public service?"

Enid smiled. "I guess that depends on your viewpoint. A lot of guys at Sweet Valley High think this is the greatest idea the Chamber of Commerce ever hatched."

"Hey!" Elizabeth protested, pretending to be angry. "Whose side are you on, anyway? Do we have a traitor in our midst?"

Enid took another sip of her drink and lifted one shoulder in a half-hearted shrug. "I'm willing to admit that I don't feel as strongly about this as you do, Liz. I mean, if we can't get the contest called off, it won't be the end of civilization as we know it. Somebody, most likely Jessica, will get a crown and bring home a few prizes and that'll be the end of it."

91

Elizabeth frowned thoughtfully and stirred her soda with her straw. "I don't think it's quite that simple," she reflected. "I think the Chamber of Commerce is exploiting the girls of Sweet Valley. It doesn't matter that the money from the pageant is going for a community swimming pool. What matters is that the girls will be earning that money with their *bodies*, not their brains." Elizabeth sighed. "And then the winner will make the circuit on local TV and radio talk shows, and of course there'll be newspaper coverage. The Chamber of Commerce will count up its profits and decide it should sponsor a pageant again next year. It could go on forever."

"Let's face it, Liz," Enid said with a sigh, "we're not talking greenhouse effect here, or the destruction of Brazilian rain forests. We're not even talking about the Miss Universe pageant. The winner won't be appearing on national TV, after all, and shaping the future of American life. She's just going to ride in a few parades and cut ribbons at bowling alleys and used-car lots."

Elizabeth grinned and shook her head. "You're hopeless," she said, but she was getting a little tired of fighting this fight herself. Some of Jessica's arguments were even starting to make a weird kind of sense. Many beauty queens *had* gone on to make their mark in the world, and

Elizabeth could certainly understand her twin's wish to be special and successful.

When Elizabeth got home later that afternoon she was in a more cheerful mood. Hearing the muted sound of a radio from the direction of the pool, Elizabeth decided to enter the house from the back. She found Jessica sunning herself beside the twinkling turquoise water. Under normal circumstances the scene would not have been unusual, but lately Jessica had been keeping a pretty hectic schedule. Elizabeth didn't know where her sister was spending her time—Jessica was so secretive these days—but whatever she was up to was time-consuming, to say the least.

Remembering all the times when she'd tried to talk to Jessica and been rebuffed, Elizabeth didn't speak to her sister as she passed her. She just opened the back door and went into the house.

Mrs. Wakefield was in the kitchen, putting the finishing touches on her special lasagna. "Hi, Liz," she said with a warm smile. "Tough day in the trenches?"

Elizabeth filled a glass with ice, then took a soda from the refrigerator. The truth was, no one seemed to care as much about the beauty pageant issue as she did. In spite of her positive words to Enid earlier, she knew most people were just not passionate, either about the pageant itself or about the Chamber of Commerce using the Sweet Valley High auditorium to hold the event.

"We're not only losing the battle," she said, sitting down in a chair at the table and pulling the anti-pageant flyers from her bag. "I think we're losing the war, too."

# Eight

"Concentrate!" Mr. Krezenski scolded, clapping his hands at Jessica as if she were a chicken he wanted to frighten away. "A dancer must *concentrate!*"

Jessica was the only student present. She bit back an angry response and went through each of the steps again.

"Passable work," Mr. Krezenski said when the music came to a fuzzy stop.

Jessica reminded herself that she would only have to endure four more killer dance lessons before the pageant. After that she could relax and enjoy being Miss Teen Sweet Valley. Whenever she wanted to give up, which was often, she thought of having her own silver car (which she would *not* let her sister borrow) and of the

95

delicious clothes she would buy on her shopping spree.

"I'm proud of you," said Mrs. Wakefield, who was waiting just inside the studio door. "You were really working hard."

Jessica was very glad her mother had come in to watch her dance instead of waiting in the car as she normally did. "Thanks," she beamed. "Think I'll win the talent segment?"

Mrs. Wakefield patted her daughter's shoulder and smiled warmly. "There's one thing I'm sure of: your dad and I will be cheering for you all the way. Aren't you going to introduce me to your teacher?"

With an eager nod, Jessica pulled her mother across the room to meet Mr. Krezenski. He was very friendly, and told Mrs. Wakefield he was looking forward to watching Jessica perform in the pageant on Saturday night.

When Jessica and Mrs. Wakefield reached the car, Jessica noticed several small, white paper bags in the back seat. A scrumptious aroma greeted her as she slid into the passenger seat.

"Chinese food," she said delightedly as she fastened her seat belt.

Mrs. Wakefield had already snapped her own belt into place and was putting the key into the ignition. "It seemed like a good day for a convenient meal. You had your dance lesson and Elizabeth stayed after school to work on some project."

A bit of Jessica's pleasure faded. No doubt Elizabeth was still working on getting the pageant canceled. And even though the big occasion was only a few days away, Jessica knew she couldn't rest easy. Once Elizabeth set her mind on a goal, she almost always succeeded. Which was another reason Jessica wanted the Miss Teen Sweet Valley title so badly. Elizabeth was the sensible one, the one who got good grades, the one who knew exactly what she wanted to do with her life. A serious limelight shortage was developing in the Wakefield family, and Jessica wanted, *needed*, her share! The pageant would be a forum for Jessica Wakefield, the whole person, to show her stuff.

"You look troubled," Mrs. Wakefield observed quietly. "Have things gotten so bad between you and Elizabeth that you can't stand to hear her name mentioned?"

Jessica twisted uncomfortably in her seat. "Liz and I can't seem to find any common ground."

"How about the fact that you're sisters?" Mrs. Wakefield suggested mildly.

Jessica was unable to think of an answer and sat silently.

Fifteen minutes later, when the Wakefield family sat down to a casual dinner of take-out Chinese food in the kitchen, Elizabeth was bright-eyed and fidgety with excitement.

"For heaven's sake, Elizabeth," Mrs. Wakefield finally prompted, "what is it?"

Jessica waited with a feeling of dread trembling in the pit of her stomach.

Elizabeth met her sister's gaze briefly, then averted her eyes to look at Mrs. Wakefield instead. "Well, in spite of our protests and petitions, we haven't been able to gather enough support to stop the pageant. So, as a last resort, I spent a couple of hours going through the rules concerning events held in the Sweet Valley High auditorium," she said after a long, tense moment. "And I think I've found a way to stop the beauty pageant, once and for all."

For a minute no one responded.

"What do you mean?" Jessica asked with quiet dignity when she could trust herself to talk. While she had been knocking herself out at Mr. Krezenski's studio, Elizabeth had been searching musty old books for musty old rules. It figured.

Elizabeth straightened her shoulders and looked squarely at her sister. "It seems no outside organization can hold a money-raising event without written consent from the school superintendent. And he's been away on a special trip to the Soviet Union, meeting with Soviet educators."

Jessica felt steam rising inside her. She was sure she was going to explode. "Great!" she cried. "Fantastic! Here I am, working harder than I ever have in my life to accomplish something I can really be proud of, something people will *notice* me for, and my own *sister* has to ruin everything! Thanks a lot, Liz!"

Only when Mr. Wakefield quietly asked her to sit down did Jessica realize she'd shot to her feet like a rocket. She sank back into her chair, still shaking with anger, and glared at her twin.

"I have to do what I think is right," Elizabeth said, her tone quiet but firm.

Jessica was too furious to speak reasonably. She excused herself, went to her room, and put on a swimsuit. She was racing from one end of the Wakefields' pool to the other, trying to vent some of her rage, when Elizabeth came to sit on the tiled edge and dangled her feet in the cool water.

Twilight was falling, and the air smelled of chlorine and the rose and lilac bushes growing nearby.

"I hope you're happy, Liz," Jessica sputtered as she paused to tread water in the middle of the pool. Droplets flew in every direction as she tossed her head.

"I haven't been happy since this whole thing started," Elizabeth replied. "Not really. What did you mean when you said you've been working harder than ever before?"

Jessica was still near tears in spite of her effort to swim away from her emotions. She glided over to the side of the pool and gripped the ladder with one hand. She looked up into Elizabeth's face.

"I've been taking dance lessons," she said, and it felt good not to be keeping the secret from Elizabeth anymore.

Elizabeth looked away for a moment. "Oh."

"Did you think I was just going to show up on pageant night, smile pretty, and hope for the best?" Jessica asked, stung by her sister's obvious surprise. "In case you haven't noticed, there are some very talented people competing for the title. Winning involves *work*, not just luck and good looks."

Elizabeth held up both of her hands. "I know, I know," she said wearily. "There's more to a beauty pageant than just being pretty."

"There is," Jessica insisted indignantly. "Amy Sutton is going to twirl her baton."

Elizabeth raised one eyebrow. "Now there's a terrifying threat," she teased.

Jessica smiled in spite of herself. Then her convictions took over again. This was her big chance, and she wasn't going to forget that. "It would be great if Amy was the only person I had to worry about. But there's Maggie. She's had all sorts of special training as an actress. And Sharon, who's been playing classical piano since she was four years old."

Elizabeth pulled one foot out of the water and began to inspect the fuchsia polish on her toenails. "I've asked this question before, and now I'm going to ask it again. Why is this pageant so important to you?"

To Jessica's way of thinking, it was enough that she had told Elizabeth about the dance lessons and her secret fear of losing to Sharon or Maggie. She was still too raw from previous battles with her sister to talk about her feelings for Frazer McConnell, her dreams of driving her own car and of choosing a glorious wardrobe at the mall, and her desire for a fabulous career.

"I just want to win, that's why it's so important," Jessica finally answered.

"But you're always winning," Elizabeth pointed out reasonably.

Jessica thought of the rule Elizabeth had found, the enforcement of which would result in the cancellation of the pageant and the cancellation of all of Jessica's hopes. "So you figured it was time to stop me, right?" she snapped. She dove back under the water and swam away.

When she surfaced again, Elizabeth was gone.

Elizabeth lay awake for a long time that night. She was heartbroken. For a while, out by the pool, it had looked as though she and Jessica might be able to reopen diplomatic relations. Then things had gone wrong again.

It wasn't that Elizabeth had changed her mind about beauty pageants; she still thought they were wrong. After all, you didn't see contests like that for men. Forget the supposed talent, forget the cute little questions the judges asked; what *really* mattered was how a girl filled out a swimsuit.

Previous arguments with Jessica churned through Elizabeth's mind. She heard her twin accusing her of being self-righteous, of wanting to make decisions for other people as well as herself. Most clearly of all, she remembered the look on Jessica's face when she had talked about her dance lessons.

There was no doubt that Jessica had been giving up a lot of her time to work on her dancing.

Elizabeth's eyes filled with tears. As much as she loved Jessica and wanted things to be right between them again, she still didn't see how she could back down on her principles.

* * *

When Elizabeth came into the kitchen the next morning, she found her father at the table, drinking coffee and reading the morning paper. He smiled when he saw her, folded the newspaper, and laid it aside.

"Want to talk?" he asked.

Elizabeth helped herself to a glass of orange juice and joined Mr. Wakefield at the table. "It's this beauty pageant thing," she said. "I've wanted to stop it from the first, and I still do, but I wasn't planning on losing my sister in the process."

Mr. Wakefield stirred his coffee. "Elizabeth, the problem here is not that you and Jessica have a difference of opinion. The difficulty comes from the way you both *react* to that problem."

"You mean you don't think I'm wrong?"

"No," Mr. Wakefield answered. "And I don't think Jessica is, either. You have a right to protest; she has an equal right to participate."

Elizabeth took another sip of her orange juice. "It sounds so simple when you put it like that, but for some reason, Jessica and I can't seem to stop fighting."

"You'll manage to work it out," her father said with quiet confidence. "Things like this sometimes take a lot of time and effort, no matter how simple they may seem on the surface."

Elizabeth nodded, then gathered up her book bag and purse and left the house to meet Todd. He pulled into the driveway as she was coming down the walk, and just seeing him lifted Elizabeth's spirits.

When they reached Sweet Valley High, Elizabeth went to the office immediately to ask for an appointment with Mr. Cooper, the principal. The secretary asked her to come back at lunchtime.

All morning Elizabeth had trouble concentrating on her classes. She kept thinking about Jessica, and about how hard her twin had worked to prepare herself for the pageant. It wasn't like Jessica to put herself out for *anything*, which meant that the title of Miss Teen Sweet Valley was something she *really* wanted.

Jessica was tense all morning. She kept expecting to hear an announcement over the school sound system that the Miss Teen Sweet Valley pageant had been postponed indefinitely.

"Did Elizabeth tell you about my dress?" Amy demanded when the two girls met near their lockers just before lunch.

Jessica held back a sigh. "No, Amy," she said. "What dress is this?"

Amy's eyes were twinkling with triumph. It was obvious she thought she had the Miss

Teen Sweet Valley crown and sash in the bag. "Only the most sophisticated, expensive gown Simple Splendor had to offer. My mother let me use her charge card to buy it. What are you wearing?"

Thinking of the beautiful pink dress at home in her closet, just waiting to dazzle the audience and the judges on pageant night, Jessica smiled happily. Even the nagging doubt that she might never get to wear it if Elizabeth had her way was no match for the glory of that dress! "Nothing special," she lied with a little shrug. "Have you worked out a baton routine?"

The girls walked along the hallway together.

"Yes," Amy answered confidently. "What are *you* going to do for the talent segment?"

Now that Elizabeth knew about her dancing, Jessica saw no point in keeping a low profile any longer. Besides, she'd worked hard. She told Amy a little about her dance number.

Amy frowned. "Are you good?" she demanded as they stopped before Jessica's classroom door.

Jessica smiled her most mischievous smile. "What do you think?" she countered.

When everyone else in her crowd was in the cafeteria having lunch, Elizabeth went to Mr. Cooper's office. He was sitting at his desk, eating a tuna sandwich and drinking coffee from a styrofoam cup.

He put down his sandwich and smiled when he noticed Elizabeth in the doorway. "Hello, Elizabeth," he said. "Please sit down and tell me what I can do for you."

Now that her chance to set things right had finally arrived, Elizabeth was unexpectedly nervous. She took the chair Mr. Cooper offered.

"Well?" the principal prompted.

"It's about the beauty pageant," she finally blurted out.

Mr. Cooper nodded. "I'm well aware of your feelings about that, Elizabeth. Your article for *The Oracle* was very well written, and you handled yourself well during the television interview. All the same, Sweet Valley High has a policy of lending its auditorium to any worthy community cause. And the Chamber of Commerce has certainly done a lot for the town in the past. A community swimming pool is only the latest plan."

Elizabeth drew in a deep breath, and let it out again. All she had to do was tell Mr. Cooper about the rule forbidding such events without written permission from the superintendent himself. Why was it so hard to do that? "Yes, well . . ."

The principal took another bite of his sandwich and waited for Elizabeth to go on.

106

Elizabeth felt like a drowning swimmer grasping for a life preserver, and her smile was probably a little on the hysterical side. "I suppose you wanted to go along on that trip to the Soviet Union," she said brightly.

Mr. Cooper looked surprised, but he nodded politely. "Yes. I hope I'll get a chance to go next year."

Elizabeth drummed the fingers of her right hand on the arm of her chair. So much for stall tactics. Mr. Cooper was still wearing a pleasant expression, but he was bound to get impatient soon enough. Besides, she was missing lunch and she was hungry.

Elizabeth tried, but she just couldn't make herself shoot down Jessica's chances at something she seemed to want so much.

"It's about *The Oracle* budget," Elizabeth said quickly. She was floundering. "We're a little low on funds, and we'd like to hold a benefit cake sale."

Mr. Cooper smiled distractedly. "I thought you said this was about the beauty pageant."

Elizabeth bit her lower lip. She was very embarrassed. "Well, only in the sense that our bake sale is kind of a community effort, too," she said lamely.

Mr. Cooper didn't look at all convinced, but he plainly wanted to get back to his sandwich and the file he'd been going over when Elizabeth first came in. "Fine, fine," he said. "Have your bake sale."

Elizabeth thanked him and dashed out of the office so fast that she almost collided with Enid when she reached the hallway.

"What did he say?" Enid asked. Earlier that day, Elizabeth had told her about her plan to get the pageant called off on a technicality.

Elizabeth looked around. She did not want anyone else to hear what she had to say. "Oh, Enid," she said in a whispered wail, clapping both hands over her face, "I couldn't do it. I couldn't tell Mr. Cooper about the rule! What's the matter with me? After all the planning, all the hard work . . ."

Enid was remarkably calm, considering how many hours she had spent marching, making signs, and getting signatures on petitions. "Because of Jessica?" she asked, putting a hand on Elizabeth's shoulder.

"Because of Jessica," Elizabeth admitted as she dropped her hands. "But I won't go to that silly pageant," she hastened to add. "From now on, Jess is strictly on her own."

"Right," said Enid with a mock-serious expression as they set out toward the cafeteria, where Elizabeth hoped to grab a quick sandwich and a piece of fruit.

"You don't believe me!" Elizabeth accused. "Well, Enid Rollins, it so happens that I have a date with Todd Saturday night. We're going to the movies."

Enid didn't seem to be paying attention. "There's Jessica right now, over at her locker. Are you going to tell her?"

"No," Elizabeth answered briskly. She'd already stretched her principles to the limit and let down all of her friends and those people of Sweet Valley who had signed petitions protesting the pageant. Jessica would have to hear the news from someone else.

# Nine

All the rest of the week, Elizabeth and Jessica did their best to avoid each other. When they did accidentally cross paths, either at home or at school, they barely spoke. Keeping silent was harder for Jessica. Every day she wondered if Elizabeth had dropped her bomb on Mr. Cooper, and if she hadn't, *why* she hadn't. But her pride just wouldn't allow her to ask.

For her part, Elizabeth wasn't angry with Jessica; she was just tired of fighting. In fact, in the days since she had gone to Mr. Cooper's office with the intention of putting an end to the Miss Teen Sweet Valley pageant once and for all, Elizabeth had done a lot of soul-searching. She was ready to admit, to herself if not yet to Jessica, that she had been just a little pigheaded about the whole thing.

Her feelings about beauty pageants hadn't changed, but this was clearly a case where the best advice was to live and let live. Elizabeth couldn't understand why she hadn't grasped that idea before.

On Saturday morning, the day of the pageant, Jessica headed down to the basement to practice her dance routine with a determination that still surprised her sister. Elizabeth went to the beach with Todd.

"Is our movie date still on?" Todd asked, sitting down on the sand next to Elizabeth. Droplets of moisture glistened on his skin, and he smelled pleasantly of fresh air and ocean water.

Elizabeth adjusted her sunglasses. She should have known Todd would pick up on her quiet, distracted mood. "Of course," she answered. "Why do you ask?"

He smiled, and Elizabeth's heart tripped into a slightly faster beat. "Come on, Liz," he said. "This is Todd you're talking to. Tonight is Jessica's pageant, and I know the Wakefields are very big on family unity."

Elizabeth sighed. "Maybe so, but we're also big on standing up for our principles. If I went with Mom and Dad, it would look as though I were putting my stamp of approval on the whole beauty contest concept."

Todd stretched out on the sand and cupped

his hands behind his head. "Some people would think that, I guess," he agreed idly. "But others would figure you were giving your stamp of approval to your *sister*, not to some concept."

"Whose side are you on, anyway?" Elizabeth demanded, poking Todd lightly in the ribs with her elbow.

He reached up to curve a finger under her chin. "Yours," he said. "Always yours."

"We're going to the movies, just as we planned," Elizabeth told him firmly. Decisively.

Todd sighed. "OK," he agreed. "I just wanted to give you an out in case you'd changed your mind."

Later that afternoon, however, when Elizabeth arrived home, she couldn't resist tapping on Jessica's bedroom door.

As usual, the place looked as though a bomb had gone off in the closet. Elizabeth almost laughed out loud when she saw Jessica standing before her mirror, wearing a bathrobe and a head full of curlers, holding a wadded-up towel like a bouquet, smiling and waving at her own reflection.

"If you came to make a last-minute effort to talk me out of going to the pageant," Jessica said, barely giving her sister a glance, "you're wasting your time. By this time tomorrow, I'll have my own car and more clothes than Lila Fowler."

Elizabeth frowned. "Your own car? Clothes? What are you talking about?"

Jessica waved one hand at her sister, as if to say she didn't have time for silly conversations. "The pageant prizes, of course," she answered.

Troubled, Elizabeth left the room. She'd read the list of prizes the various merchants of Sweet Valley had donated for the pageant, and she didn't think there had been mention of a car.

Elizabeth went to her closet and started to search through her clothes for just the right outfit to wear to the movies that night with Todd. But she just couldn't concentrate. She kept thinking of Jessica's remarks about the contest prizes. She hoped her twin wasn't building herself up for a big disappointment with a lot of unrealistic expectations.

She started toward the bathroom door, meaning to cut through and confront Jessica again, but halfway across the room she stopped herself. She was building herself up for a big disappointment if she thought Jessica would want to listen to anything she had to say. And Elizabeth had no desire for another blowup with her sister.

Elizabeth went back to her room, sat down

113

at her desk, rolled a piece of paper into her typewriter, and began working on next week's column for *The Oracle*.

Jessica was so full of excitement that she could barely stand still, and her stomach was so jumpy that she couldn't choke down either lunch or dinner. She was so close to her dreams, she could almost reach out and touch them!

Taking the beautiful evening gown she'd borrowed from Simple Splendor from the closet, Jessica carefully placed it in a garment bag she'd borrowed from her mother. She packed her white leotard, tights, and dancing slippers into a big canvas tote along with the taped music for her performance.

Steven had casually mentioned that Frazer was coming to the pageant with him. He said that the two of them had plans for later, but Jessica was convinced that Frazer wouldn't want to leave her side once he'd really seen her in action.

She was blissfully happy. Everything was falling into place.

Jessica took a long, leisurely bubble bath, during which she could hear the keys of Elizabeth's typewriter click-clacking away on the other side of the door. Didn't that girl ever rest?

Jessica put her twin out of her mind and imagined herself picking Frazer up at the dorm in her shiny new silver convertible. She probably wouldn't be wearing her crown and sash when that particular dream came true, but it was OK in the fantasy.

Smiling happily, Jessica finished her bath and proceeded to put on her makeup and style her hair. It was all a little like the story of Cinderella, she reflected, except for that silly business about the glass slipper. Jessica had no intention of leaving the ball without the prince firmly wrapped around her little finger. Her own private "coach" was already waiting for her at one of the Sweet Valley car dealerships, and nobody was going to wave a wand at midnight and turn it into a pumpkin. Not even Elizabeth.

At seven o'clock that night, Mr. and Mrs. Wakefield drove her to the auditorium at Sweet Valley High.

"Good luck, sweetheart," Mr. Wakefield said when they left her at the door. He kissed her lightly on the cheek. "We'll be cheering for you."

Mrs. Wakefield nodded her agreement, then hugged Jessica. "See you after the pageant," she said.

There were several dressing rooms behind the stage, but the contestants, girls from high schools throughout the community, were all crowded into one. Jessica made her way through billowing dresses, shimmering costumes, hair dryers, and suitcases to find the dressing table with her name on it. The first part of the pageant would consist of an evening gown competition, so Jessica carefully unwrapped her glorious dress and went behind an improvised curtain to slip it on.

Amy, who was wearing a spectacular full-skirted creation covered in black sequins, fastened Jessica's zipper for her.

"Nice dress," Amy said casually, but her forehead was wrinkled and there was a fretful look in her eyes.

Jessica could afford to be generous. From the looks of things, she was pretty much a shoo-in for the Miss Teen Sweet Valley title. "Thanks. Yours is great, too." Secretly Jessica thought the gown was too sophisticated for Amy; she looked like a little girl playing dress-up. The winking sequins were enough to blind a person. "What are you wearing for your talent number?"

Amy riffled through some garments hanging on one of the portable racks borrowed from the drama club's costume department, and held up a cute blue satin outfit that looked like a truncated tuxedo. The lapels glistened with matching sparkles, and so did the band around the coordinating top hat.

Jessica swallowed and thought of her plain white leotard. Then she reminded herself that when it came to clothes, simpler was always better. Didn't Elizabeth always say that? Jessica turned up her smile a few watts.

"I can't do it," Elizabeth told Todd when he came to pick her up for movies that night. "I've got to be there for Jess, no matter how much I hate beauty contests."

Todd didn't look the least bit surprised. In fact, he grinned. "No problem. We can always take in a matinee tomorrow. Come on, Liz. I'll drop you off at the auditorium. I could stand to put in a little extra studying for that history test anyway."

"Thanks," Elizabeth answered, a little uncertainly. First she had backed down from a chance to accomplish her goal of stopping the pageant entirely, and now she was going back on her vow not to attend the thing. Where would it all end?

When they reached Sweet Valley High, Elizabeth said goodbye to Todd and hurried up to the impromptu box office to buy a ticket. She stood at the back of the crowded auditorium and scanned the audience. Finally she managed to spot her family seated near the front.

Elizabeth couldn't hold back a little smile

when she saw that her mother had saved her a place. Sometimes, Elizabeth thought, Todd and her parents knew her better than she knew herself.

After greeting her parents, Steven, and Frazer with whispered hellos, Elizabeth settled into the seat next to her mother. People were still filing in, the lights were up, and the place buzzed with conversation.

"How did you know I'd change my mind?" Elizabeth asked as she smoothed her program on her lap.

Mrs. Wakefield smiled. "I'm psychic," she teased. "Next week, I plan to go into business reading palms."

"But I really *meant* it when I said I wasn't coming tonight," Elizabeth insisted. And it was true. She'd had no intention of showing her face at an event she'd condemned with so much enthusiasm.

"I know," Mrs. Wakefield said with a nod and a distinct twinkle in her eyes. "But when it came right down to it, you just weren't able to ignore something that was so important to your sister."

Elizabeth sighed. "No," she said, looking wistfully at the curtain. "I know it's crazy, because we live in the same house and everything, but I've *missed* Jess these past few weeks. It's as if she's been away or something."

118

"In a way, she has," Mrs. Wakefield replied. "I've never seen Jessica so determined to succeed at anything. She spent every spare hour practicing her dancing at Mr. Krezenski's studio."

Just then the school orchestra started to play and the lights went down. The audience settled back as the stage curtains whisked aside and Mr. Cooper came out with a microphone in one hand.

"As you know," he began, "the Chamber of Commerce is sponsoring this, our first annual Miss Teen Sweet Valley pageant. . . ."

Elizabeth winced at the words "first annual," then forced herself to listen to the program.

One by one the entrants' names were announced, and they swept onstage in magnificent, glittering dresses. Elizabeth recognized several sophomores, as well as several juniors and seniors. There were girls from other schools, too, but Elizabeth's attention was soon focused on the three most obvious contenders: Jessica, Sharon Jefferson, the pianist with a hearing impairment, and Maggie Simmons, the trained actress. Amy Sutton looked very nice in her gown, and Elizabeth knew she was a pretty good baton twirler, but there was something vital lacking, some strength or personality that the other three had in abundance.

Elizabeth folded her arms as the questions began.

"If you could be any room in the house," Mr. Cooper asked of Amy, reading from an index card, "which one would you be?

Elizabeth rolled her eyes and glanced at her mother, who only smiled.

Amy pondered the question seriously, as though it had been put to her by a committee of senators and representatives. Then she smiled brightly. "I guess I'd be the living room, because that's where we keep our stereo and our big-screen TV. It's the most fun room in the house!"

Elizabeth swallowed a giggle.

The audience clapped politely, and Jessica stepped up to center stage. She looked like a princess from a fairy tale in that remarkable dress, with its trim of little pearls. In spite of everything that had passed between them in the past several weeks, Elizabeth felt a twinge of real pride in her sister.

"If you were elected President of the United States," Mr. Cooper began, again consulting one of his cards, "what is the first thing you would do after taking office?"

Jessica's smile had more electricity than all the stage lights combined. "I would see that stricter laws were made to protect the environment," she replied, "and I'd make certain something was done to help the homeless."

The applause for Jessica was overwhelming,

and Elizabeth clapped, too, even though she knew the first thing President Jessica Wakefield would do would be to redecorate the White House.

Jessica changed into her white leotard, tights, and dance slippers, and pulled her hair back into a sleek dancer's bun.

Amy was the first to go on, and Jessica watched from the wings as her friend performed. There was no getting around it: Amy was good with the baton, but she didn't have enough stage presence to keep everyone's attention.

Jessica searched the rows for her family and Frazer, but the auditorium was so dark, she couldn't make out a single familiar face. Her mind shifted unexpectedly to Elizabeth, who had chosen to go to a movie with Todd rather than to attend the pageant, and Jessica felt a pang of hurt. This was one of those times when she really needed the support of her family. *Everyone* in her family.

Maggie came on and did one of Juliet's scenes from *Romeo and Juliet*. She wore a spectacular green velvet dress from last year's production of *The Taming of the Shrew*. Her performance was stunning, and Jessica began to get really nervous.

121

When Sharon came out to play the baby grand piano that had been rolled onstage a few moments after Maggie's scene ended, things went from bad to worse—from Jessica's point of view, at least.

Sharon's fingers flew gracefully over the keys, bringing forth music that seemed to flow from some better, brighter place on earth. When the Mozart composition was over, the audience sat in startled silence for a few seconds, then burst into thunderous applause.

For one terrible moment Jessica was afraid the audience was actually going to stand up and cheer for Sharon. In the end, though, the members of the audience remained in their seats and the piano was rolled offstage again.

Jessica tried to put the last two performances out of her mind. It was her turn to perform and Mr. Krezenski had drilled her over and over again on the importance of total concentration. She knew her teacher was out front, along with her parents and Steven and Frazer, and she wanted them all to be proud of her. And she wanted to be proud of herself.

Jessica was introduced, the familiar music began, and she danced gracefully across the stage. As she twirled and whirled through the carefully practiced steps, her heart seemed to fly a few inches above her head. She was wonderful, she was magnificent, she was elegance itself.

Then toward the end of her number, disaster struck. Jessica tripped and landed on her knees, staining her white tights with stage dust. The audience gasped with startled sympathy, then went still in shared embarrassment.

On the verge of sobbing, her smile frozen on her face, Jessica forced herself to finish the dance. But the moment it was over and she had reached the safety of the wings, she fled.

Pushing past the advisors and the other contestants, Jessica grabbed her bag from the pageant contestants' room and hid out in one of the unused dressing rooms. She changed into shorts and a T-shirt, making frantic plans all the while to escape before she had to face anyone. Tears of humiliation trickled down her cheeks.

# Ten

Elizabeth felt the impact of Jessica's fall as sharply as if she'd struck the floor herself. She was already in the aisle, headed toward the door at stage left, before the performance ended.

Applause pounded against Elizabeth's eardrums as she searched the hallway for her sister. The other girls waiting backstage, along with various mothers and advisors, didn't seem to notice Elizabeth at all.

Elizabeth saw Jessica dart out of the largest dressing room and into a smaller one down the hall, and she followed, slowing her pace a little to give her sister time to pull herself together.

There was only one dim light burning in the room. Elizabeth immediately heard the sound of Jessica's soft, furious sobs, and felt a corresponding ache in her own heart.

"Jess?"

"Go away!" Jessica sniffled. Already dressed in shorts and a top, she was stuffing her white dance costume into her canvas bag. "I'm in no mood to watch you gloat! And what are you doing here, anyway? I thought you weren't coming."

Elizabeth stood her ground and folded her arms stubbornly. But her voice was gentle. "I *had* to come tonight, Jess. And I *didn't* come in here now to say 'I told you so.' You were terrific tonight, and I think you should go back and finish the pageant, just the way you finished your dance."

Jessica sniffed again and rubbed her face with the back of both hands, streaking her eye makeup. "No way," she replied as she shook her head. "I made a fool of myself out there. There's nothing I can do but leave town. I'll make a new start somewhere else, maybe change my name—"

"Oh, please," Elizabeth interrupted with good-natured impatience. "It's not that big a deal. Everybody makes mistakes, and besides, you still have a good chance of winning."

Jessica gave a bitter laugh. "Oh, right. After Maggie's Oscar-winning performance and Sharon's fabulous piano concert! The judges are going to give me the title for Best Fall on Her Face in the Middle of a Number!"

Elizabeth deliberately blocked the door so Jessica couldn't get past. "According to the program," she went on calmly, as though Jessica hadn't spoken at all, "the infamous swimsuit competition is next. Why don't you wash your face, put on that knockout suit you swiped from me, and go out there and show these people just how good a California girl can look?"

Jessica's mouth dropped open. "Is that *you* talking, Liz?" she asked after a long moment. "You hate beauty pageants, *particularly* the swimsuit competition!"

"That's true," Elizabeth agreed. "But I care a whole lot about you, Jessica. I don't think I realized just how much until things got so bad between us. I've really missed you these past few weeks."

Jessica turned to one of the sinks and splashed her face with cold water. "You've had a change of heart," she said between splashes. "Well, that's great. But *I* wouldn't go out there again for anything."

Elizabeth knew when Jessica meant what she said, and she knew when her sister was making a big mistake. Elizabeth also knew she'd be wasting her breath if she kept trying to persuade Jessica to take the risk and finish what she had begun out there on the stage.

Jessica pushed past Elizabeth and left the dressing room.

Elizabeth's attention was riveted on the canvas dance bag Jessica had left behind. Elizabeth guessed it contained everything Jessica needed for the pageant except, of course, the billowy pink dress from never-never land. Inspiration struck her. And so did sheer panic.

"I'm not thinking this," Elizabeth told the empty dressing room sternly. "I cannot be thinking this!"

But even as she spoke she was already opening the bag, stripping off her clothes, and pulling on the turquoise suit. Thanks to a day at the beach with Todd, her skin was tanned to a golden tone, and a few strokes of a brush would give her hair the same tousled look as Jessica's.

"What are you doing?" Elizabeth demanded of her own image in the mirror as she styled her hair to look like Jessica's and made subtle changes in her makeup. "Have you gone crazy?"

All Elizabeth really knew was that she couldn't let her twin remember this night as a humiliating defeat. "For the next fifteen minutes," she said to her reflection, "I'm Jessica Wakefield. Where are those high heels?"

Elizabeth found the heels, slipped them on, and hurried out the door.

There was no sign of Jessica in the hallway, though Elizabeth hoped her sister was hanging around somewhere. Elizabeth drew a deep breath, strolled down the hall, and blended in easily with the other contestants, who were, as usual, too absorbed in their own concerns to notice anything out of the ordinary.

Mrs. Bates, a volunteer who was one of the pageant advisors, patted Elizabeth on the shoulder. "It's very brave of you to stick this out until the bitter end, Jessica," she said sympathetically. "The show must go on, mustn't it?"

Amy's smile contained only triumph. She looked tan and fit in her snow-white swimsuit. "Don't worry, Jess," she whispered. "I'll let you help me pick out all those new clothes on the shopping spree!"

Elizabeth raised her eyebrows but offered no comment. When she glanced back over one shoulder, she saw Jessica peeking around the edge of an old prop. Good.

Sharon made her way through the group of girls and smiled at Elizabeth. Her hearing aid was all but hidden beneath her attractive hairstyle, and, like Amy, she looked terrific in her suit. Her voice was slightly garbled because of her handicap, but her manner was warm and pleasant.

"You did really well, Jessica," she said sincerely.

Elizabeth felt a surge of warmth for this friendly girl. "Thanks, Sharon," she said.

Maggie Simmons touched her shoulder with

the light, instinctive grace of a gifted actress. "I made a couple of mistakes out there myself," she said. "Don't let it worry you."

Along with the warmth, Elizabeth felt a little bit of shame, too. She'd not only judged beauty pageants too harshly, it seemed she'd judged the contestants too harshly as well. She could see now that most of these girls were very nice. They just happened to have opinions that differed from hers.

"Good luck," Elizabeth said, her voice tight with sudden emotion. "I wish everyone could win."

Moments later, though, when she found herself walking the length of the stage in her turquoise swimsuit and Jessica's high-heeled white satin shoes, Elizabeth was wishing something else entirely. She wished she was on another planet.

As the audience oohed and aahed and clapped, color surged into Elizabeth's cheeks. Here she was, doing the very thing she'd made such a point of putting down: strutting half-naked down a runway for the entertainment of strangers! What would Todd and Enid and the others say if they knew it was *Elizabeth* Wakefield prancing around that stage, not Jessica?

By sheer force of will, Elizabeth managed to get through the swimsuit segment of the contest. While the other girls were rushing to change back into their evening dresses, Elizabeth slipped back into the shadowy room where Jessica had been hiding earlier.

Jessica was full of new energy, and her cheeks were flushed pink. She had fixed her hair and repaired her makeup, and she was again wearing that wonderful pink dress.

She hugged Elizabeth gently, her blue-green eyes sparkling with fresh tears. But this time, she looked happy.

"I was in the wings and saw what you did, Liz," she said. "Thank you so much!"

Elizabeth was already urging her sister toward the door. "Don't think I'm going to say 'anytime,' Jess, because I'm not," she teased. "If I never have to do that again, it will be too soon."

Jessica laughed, dried her eyes carefully so she wouldn't smudge her makeup, and hurried out to join the other girls on stage.

Elizabeth changed back into her own clothes and waited until she was certain the contestants were all onstage again. Then she walked casually out to her seat in the auditorium and sat down again.

"I see she's all right," Mrs. Wakefield whispered, referring to Jessica, who was now standing onstage with the others, her glowing face showing no trace of the tears she'd shed before.

Elizabeth's cheeks were still pink from her

mortifying moments of glory on that stage, wearing her own swimsuit and Jessica's identity. "You know Jess," she whispered back. "Nothing can keep her down for long."

Jessica's heart fluttered when Mr. Cooper gestured for a drum roll from the orchestra and then said, "We will now announce the finalists for the title of Miss Teen Sweet Valley."

The suspense was unbearable as the principal opened an envelope, took out the paper inside, unfolded it, and pretended to think seriously about the contents.

"Ladies and gentlemen, our finalists are . . ."

Another drum roll, only slightly louder than the pounding of Jessica's heart. She no longer believed she was the sure winner. In addition to having answered their questions with intelligence, Sharon and Maggie had both given flawless performances. *She* had fallen on her face! In fact, she wouldn't be up here onstage at all if it hadn't been for Elizabeth.

"Miss Sharon Jefferson!"

The audience applauded long and loud as Sharon stepped forward, with a beaming smile, to stand alongside Mr. Cooper.

"Miss Maggie Simmons!"

Again, the walls and floor seemed to shake. Maggie gracefully took her place next to Sharon, and Jessica tossed a sidelong glance to Amy. Her friend looked so anxious, so hopeful, that for one crazy second Jessica almost wanted her to win. Of course, all the girls were nervous, their smiles tense and eager.

"Miss Jessica Wakefield!"

Jessica was stunned. She even thought for a moment that she had only imagined hearing her name called. Then her natural confidence kicked in and she stepped forward. The first thought that came to her was how impressed Frazer must be. He was probably planning to cancel his previous plans and ask to take her home.

With the exception of the three finalists and Mr. Cooper, everyone left the stage.

"More questions!" Mr. Cooper said as he took another sheaf of index cards from the pocket of his coat.

Jessica, Sharon, and Maggie each smiled, and the audience tittered anxiously, as though Mr. Cooper had made a joke.

"Miss Simmons," he said, turning to Maggie. "If you were in charge of the frog-jumping contest at the state fair, and one of your duties was to kiss the winner, what would you do?"

Jessica silently congratulated herself on not having gotten that particular question.

Maggie didn't miss a beat. "Why, I'd kiss him, of course," she drawled, "and hope he'd turn into a handsome prince."

The crowd was delighted. They laughed and clapped, and Jessica began to feel shaky again.

"Miss Jefferson," Mr. Cooper went on, careful to look Sharon in the face as he spoke so that she could read his lips, "what would you do if you'd just become engaged to a young man, and you went to have your engagement ring sized and found out the diamond was a fake?"

Jessica could just imagine how Elizabeth was reacting to that question—with a smirk. But let Elizabeth smirk all she wanted. She was the kind of sister a person could count on when the chips were down.

Sharon considered the query without giving any indication that she thought it was silly. "I guess I'd call off the engagement, not because the diamond wasn't real, but because my fiancé felt he couldn't be honest with me. That would mean something was very wrong with our relationship."

Again, the spectators applauded enthusiastically.

Jessica could see her shiny new convertible driving away into the sunset. Without her.

"Miss Wakefield."

Jessica took a deep breath, turned her smile up a few degrees, and stepped forward. She made sure her expression was eager and expectant as she waited for her question.

"Name the person who has had the greatest

133

impact on your life, other than either of your parents."

Jessica didn't have to think about the question for very long, but she was silent for several moments, concentrating on the mood she wanted to project. "That would have to be my sister, Elizabeth," she said, speaking so softly that Mr. Cooper held the microphone closer to her mouth. "We're identical twins, and whenever I've really needed somebody, Liz has always been there for me."

In the split second between her answer and the audience's warm response, Jessica caught sight of Elizabeth, her parents, Steven, and Frazer, all looking up proudly at her. They seemed to stand out in sharp relief, though she hadn't been able to find them before.

She saw smiles break over their faces, saw them begin to clap. The audience joined in a second later with more applause. Everything seemed to be happening in slow motion, as in some wonderful, exciting movie.

Jessica's heart pounded with excitement and, hiding one hand in the folds of her long, full skirt, she crossed her fingers for luck.

# Eleven

The moment of truth had arrived.

Jessica, Maggie, and Sharon held hands as they waited with dazzling smiles for the names of the runners-up to be announced.

There was a dramatic drum roll as Mr. Cooper slowly opened the envelope that had been handed to him by one of the judges.

"Ladies and gentlemen," Mr. Cooper said, with appropriate fanfare, "I present to you the second runner-up in the first annual Miss Teen Sweet Valley competition. Miss Maggie Simmons!"

There was more applause as Maggie hugged both Jessica and Sharon and stepped back, waiting with the others to hear the next name called.

"The first runner-up," Mr. Cooper went on at his leisure, "will fill in for Miss Teen Sweet Valley on those occasions when she is not able to fulfill her obligations." He consulted the paper in his hand again, as though he'd forgotten the order of the names written there, and the audience shifted restlessly.

Jessica's heart was beating so hard it practically deafened her.

"The first runner-up, ladies and gentlemen," Mr. Cooper finally proceeded to say, "for the title of Miss Teen Sweet Valley, is Sharon Jefferson!"

For a moment Jessica just stood there in total shock. Then it hit her. *She had won!*

"Now I present to you, ladies and gentlemen," Mr. Cooper said graciously, as the long-dreamed-of crown was placed on Jessica's head, "our very own *Miss Teen Sweet Valley— Jessica Wakefield!*"

Through a haze of happy tears Jessica saw the people in the audience stand, saw them clapping and cheering. Her mother and father looked so pleased and proud, and Elizabeth was applauding with as much excitement as anyone. Steven was grinning up at her and so was Frazer.

Mr. Cooper was naming the prizes she'd won, but for once Jessica couldn't think about them. She was in a dream state, a happy sleepwalker.

One by one, all the other girls in the pageant came back on stage to congratulate her.

While Amy looked disappointed, her smile was genuine. "Good work, Jess," she said.

Jessica could afford to be generous, now that her weeks of hard work and planning had finally paid off. "Thanks, Amy," she answered. "Your baton routine was a knockout, and you really looked good tonight."

Surprisingly, the warmest words of congratulations came from Maggie and Sharon. They both seemed genuinely thrilled that Jessica had won. She had to admit, to herself at least, that she wouldn't have been able to lose as gracefully as they did, particularly after having come so close to victory.

During the next half-hour, Jessica was in a daze. Flash-bulbs went off in her face, people shouted congratulations, reporters from the local news media pelted her with questions.

As her head began to clear, however, Jessica started to think thoughts she didn't particularly want to think. She remembered Maggie's and Sharon's perfect performances, and her own fall in the middle of her dance number.

When it came right down to it, Maggie and Sharon hadn't looked all that bad in their swimsuits, either, and they'd answered the questions Mr. Cooper put to them with intelligence, poise, and wit.

A nervous flutter settled in the pit of Jessica's stomach. Was it possible that Elizabeth had been right all along? Had Jessica won the pageant simply because she was the prettiest of the three? If that were true, Jessica reflected, it would take a lot of fun out of the winning. After all, she'd worked hard on her dancing, and she was bright. Much as she loved being the center of attention, she certainly didn't want to be valued *only* for her looks.

People continued to mill around, pushing close to her and shaking her hand. Jessica began to wish for a breath of fresh air. When was Frazer going to come up and ask if he could take her home?

Mr. and Mrs. Wakefield finally made their way through the crowd. Each of them gave Jessica a hug and a kiss on the cheek, and she knew they were proud of her.

Elizabeth smiled, her eyes twinkling as she took in the sparkling rhinestones on Jessica's head. "Well, you did it, Princess Jessica," she said. "You've got your crown."

Actually the "crown" was another small, secret disappointment to Jessica. It was pretty, but it was really more of a tiara than a crown, nothing like the stunning creations beauty queens were awarded on television. Jessica returned her sister's smile.

"Thanks, Liz," she said. She was thanking her sister for more than her congratulations, but of course Jessica wasn't about to mention what Elizabeth had done for her during the swimsuit competition. Not in front of all these people! The tiara may have been a disappointment, but she wasn't about to forfeit it for anything!

Steven gave Jessica a brotherly kiss on the forehead. "You were sensational, Jess," he said.

Jessica turned her eyes eagerly to Frazer, expecting to see adoration in his face, and was let down to find that he wasn't even *looking* at her. He was studying the ceiling of the auditorium, and if anything, he seemed bored and anxious to leave.

Jessica was devastated. She'd worked like a slave, partly for the fabulous prizes, partly for the public notice, but also to get this particular guy's attention. And it seemed now that all her efforts had been for nothing. Frazer *still* didn't know she was alive!

Jessica was distracted from these disturbing thoughts by the appearance of Mr. Krezenski. He was dressed in a nice dark suit, and his white hair had been carefully combed. He smiled as he took Jessica's hand and shook it.

"You were very professional, Miss Wakefield," he said.

His praise gave Jessica a roller-coaster sensation in the pit of her stomach. First Frazer's reaction had brought her low, then her dance instructor had sent her soaring again with a few supportive words.

Jessica nodded her thanks, and Mr. Krezenski moved on through the crowd.

"Let's all go out and have some pizza to celebrate," Mr. Wakefield suggested when things finally settled down.

"Frazer and I have dates, Dad," Steven said, sending his sister's mood plunging again without even knowing it. "But thanks anyway."

Steven and Frazer hurried off the stage and up one of the aisles. Frazer had actually looked *relieved* to be making an escape! Jessica fought back tears. It was crazy. She had a crown on her head and a sash that said MISS TEEN SWEET VALLEY in big, glittering letters, a whole slew of great prizes, and still she felt like a loser.

Only Elizabeth seemed to notice that Jessica was hurt. She squeezed her sister's hand once, offering silent reassurance.

When the Wakefields arrived at Guido's for a celebration pizza, Jessica's spirits rose a little. Her crown and sash and the wonderful pink dress caused quite a stir. The attention she got went a long way toward making her feel better.

When they were all seated, Mrs. Wakefield scanned the back of the pageant program and said with a pleased smile, "The prizes are terrific. You've won a lot of nice things, Jessica."

Jessica smiled, still conscious of the admiring stares of the other people having late-night pizza. She thought of her silver car and her beautiful new wardrobe. Why, there were probably a few prizes she didn't even know about!

"Read the list, Alice," Mr. Wakefield said.

Jessica thought Elizabeth looked a little uncomfortable at that moment, but she put the idea out of her head. The twins' relationship was back to normal again, and if there was one thing Jessica knew for certain about Elizabeth, it was that she was never jealous of other people's good fortune.

"Well," Mrs. Wakefield began, "there's a haircut at the new styling salon at the mall, a month's free bowling at Al's Alley, a set of encyclopedias, a twenty-five-dollar gift certificate from Things for Girls, ten free movie rentals at Quick-dash, and a cash prize of one hundred dollars."

For a moment Jessica sat there in shock. She saw Elizabeth look away.

"Let me see that, please," Jessica said crisply as she reached for the program. A rising tide of panic was tightening her throat. Encyclopedias? A haircut? *Bowling?* Where was the free wardrobe from Simple Splendor, the ten-thousand-dollar check?

As she scanned the humble list of prizes, Jessica's heart fell. All that work, all that hoping and planning and dreaming, and what had she gotten for it? The realization that her sister had been right about beauty pageants ignoring the whole woman, a total lack of interest from the guy she had hoped to impress, and a bunch of second-rate, dusty merchandise.

If her mother and father hadn't been watching her with such excitement, Jessica would have burst into tears right then and there. Here she had been chosen Miss Teen Sweet Valley and yet it was turning out to be the most dismal night of her life!

Jessica put on a good front for the rest of the dinner, and it wasn't until she was alone in her room later that evening that she let her true feelings show. Too angry to cry, she threw things, stomped around the floor in a circle, then battered the bed with one of her pillows.

There was a light rap at the bathroom door, and then Elizabeth peeked around the doorway. "I'm here to help you drown your sorrows," she said, coming in with two cans of diet soda and two glasses clinking with ice. "I take it you were expecting something else in the way of prizes?"

Jessica took one of the cans of soda and a

glass, shoved some things off the bed, and sat. Elizabeth, who had changed into a cotton nightshirt, took a seat on the floor, cross-legged.

"Oh, Liz," Jessica wailed. She set her soda and glass down at her feet, and then flung herself backward on the mattress and beat at it with both fists. "I feel like such an idiot. There were all these wild rumors flying around about the prizes, and I *believed* them."

"You aren't the first person whose expectations have gotten a little out of hand, Jess," Elizabeth said practically. "Let's face it, being Miss Teen Sweet Valley is not exactly a bad deal. You'll be something of a local celebrity."

At the word "celebrity," Jessica sat bolt upright. "You really think so?"

Elizabeth smiled. "Sure I do. You'll probably be invited to appear on TV again."

Stars began to dance in front of Jessica's eyes once more. She might still be discovered by a Hollywood director or a modeling agent, and even if she hadn't exactly made a hit with Frazer McConnell, there had to be a lot of *other* college guys out there who would be thrilled to date a beauty queen! Maybe the whole thing wasn't such a loss after all.

After pouring her soda into her glass, Elizabeth took a sip. "If you don't mind my asking— again—just exactly what was it you expected from this pageant?"

143

Jessica sighed and reached for her own soda. "Well, I really *did* want the recognition, you know, for my career. And I *did* want the prizes. But what I wanted most of all . . ." Jessica paused and then hurried on. "I thought Frazer would fall head over heels for me if I just had a crown and a sash." She nodded toward those much-yearned-for items, which were now lying on her dresser top.

"Frazer? Steven's friend?"

Jessica nodded. "I'm ready to start dating older guys, Liz," she confided. "The trouble is, they don't seem to be ready for me."

Elizabeth grinned. "Very few people are," she teased. And then her expression was serious again. "Jess, when the time is right, college guys will be beating down the front door."

Her lip extended in a pretend pout, Jessica quipped, "Yeah, and they'll probably be looking for you." And then she reached back, grabbed a pillow, and hurled it at her sister in mock fury.

It was business as usual with the Wakefield twins.

# Twelve

Jessica had trouble meeting her mother's eyes. "So anyway, as soon as I get the prize money from the pageant I'll pay back part of what I owe you for the dance lessons. I guess the rest will have to come out of my allowance."

Mrs. Wakefield put her hand under her daughter's chin and lifted it. "What did you learn from all this?" she asked gently.

"That there's a big difference between rumor and reality," Jessica answered with a sheepish smile.

Her mother laughed and hugged Jessica. "Most of the time there definitely is," she agreed. She glanced toward the beautiful pageant dress, once again wrapped in protective plastic. "Taking the gown back?"

Jessica nodded. Her hopes of keeping the dress and paying for it out of the prize money were no more, of course. "Yes, as soon as the mall opens."

"It was very nice of the manager to let you borrow it," Mrs. Wakefield said.

Jessica shrugged. "I convinced her it would be good advertising," she said. "And I guess it was."

Mrs. Wakefield nodded, poured coffee for herself and Mr. Wakefield, and left the kitchen.

Jessica picked up the dress along with her purse and car keys and headed for the Fiat, which was parked in the driveway. Just as she was about to get behind the wheel, Frazer McConnell pulled in.

"Steven isn't home," she told Frazer. Her heart raced a little when he stopped beside her car and bent to look in at her, his muscular arms resting against the lower edge of the window.

He smiled that blinding, white-fire smile of his. "I know," he said. "Actually, I stopped by because I wanted to see you."

Jessica's heart shimmied into her throat and pounded there, like some jungle drum gone berserk. "You did?"

Frazer nodded, and his blond hair caught the bright morning light. "The truth is, I've been wanting to ask you out for a long time," he said seriously. "But I held back because, well, you're my buddy's sister and everything."

*If he calls me Elizabeth,* Jessica thought wildly, *I'm going to jump off the nearest bridge.*

She waited.

"Maybe we could take in a movie next Friday night?" Frazer pressed.

Jessica decided to play it cool. And she still wanted some indication that he didn't think he was asking Elizabeth out. "Well, I don't know. I mean, if you're just doing this because I'm Miss Teen Sweet Valley . . ." She held her breath, watching for a frown or some other expression of confusion.

Instead, he flashed that million-megawatt grin. "No. I've really wanted to ask you out for a long time. It just took me a while to work up the courage."

Jessica rewarded him with one of her own high-voltage smiles. "See you next Friday night, then," she said.

"Seven-thirty?"

Jessica nodded. Frazer grinned again, went back to his own car, and drove away.

The way Jessica was feeling, she could have *floated* to the mall. She had a date with a college guy, and all her friends were going to be wild with envy when they got a look at Frazer.

Jessica headed for Simple Splendor, where she handed over the dress, thanked the man-

147

ager sincerely for letting her wear it in the pageant, and left. Giving up the fairy-tale gown hurt only a little.

After that, she drove by the dance studio on the off chance that Mr. Krezenski might be there. She knew he practically lived in that long, mirrored room.

He was there, even though it was Sunday.

The white-haired instructor was sitting on his solitary stool, listening to music with his eyes closed, when Jessica walked in.

"Miss Wakefield," he said with a little nod. There was something of his old, brusque manner in his voice and bearing.

"I guess you know I won't be continuing with my lessons," Jessica told him quietly. "I don't have time, between cheerleading practice and my new responsibilities as Miss Teen Sweet Valley."

Mr. Krezenski watched Jessica with wise eyes. "I am not surprised by this news, Miss Wakefield," he said. "But may I say that I think it is a pity you have lost interest in the dance. You have a very significant talent."

Jessica's cheeks were warm. "I fell," she reminded him, reliving that awful, humiliating moment at the pageant as she spoke. "You were there. You saw me."

Mr. Krezenski nodded, chuckled, and stared at something Jessica couldn't see. "I know what it is to take a fall and be embarrassed, Miss Wakefield," he said, in his stern and old-fashioned way. "I once landed on my nose, you see, while performing for the queen of England."

Jessica's eyes opened wide as she tried to imagine the glory and disgrace of such an experience. "You danced for the queen? Wow!"

"There, you see?" Mr. Krezenski chided her good-naturedly, wagging one bent finger. "It is not the failure that one focuses on, but the fact that I, Alexi Krezenski, once danced for the queen herself!" He paused to rub his chin and remember. "Afterwards, Her Royal Highness shook my hand and told me I was made of the very finest stuff because I did not quit in the face of defeat."

Jessica thought she was about to get a lecture for giving up her dance lessons when she showed such great promise, but she was wrong.

Mr. Krezenski held out one hand to her. "You, too, are made of fine stuff, Miss Wakefield. When you fell, you did not flee from the stage in tears, as many young girls would surely have done. You *finished the dance*." Mr. Krezenski shook her hand, and Jessica listened in surprise. "If you take away nothing else from these lessons," Mr. Krezenski concluded, "I hope you will always remember that one thing. You must always finish the dance."

Jessica didn't trust herself to talk. Her throat

was tight and she could feel tears gathering behind her eyes. Jessica nodded, then turned and hurried out. She hoped Mr. Krezenski understood that she had come back to thank him.

Elizabeth sighed into the telephone receiver Sunday night. "I'm sorry, Enid. But I raised the subject of a bake sale to benefit *The Oracle*, and Mr. Cooper agreed. Now I have no choice but to follow through on it."

By the tone of Enid's voice, Elizabeth knew her friend was smiling. "Well, Liz, I guess as your friend, my choices are limited, too. I'll have to help."

"Thanks," Elizabeth said. She was relieved. She wouldn't have blamed Enid if she hadn't wanted anything to do with another of her projects. The anti-pageant campaign, after all, had turned out to be a whole lot of work for nothing. Then again, maybe it hadn't. Maybe they had gotten a few people thinking about the beauty-pageant mentality. And that was worth something. "Meet you at our lockers before class tomorrow. It's my turn to take the Fiat, so I'll leave early. Jess said she would catch a ride with Lila."

"I'll be there," Enid promised. "We ought to

be able to map out some kind of strategy before the first-period bell rings.''

"You're the best friend anybody ever had," Elizabeth said, and she meant it.

"I know," Enid agreed in lofty tones. Then she giggled.

Elizabeth pulled into the school parking lot bright and early Monday morning. The area was empty except for a few teachers' cars.

As Elizabeth walked toward the main building, she noticed a lone runner doing laps on the track. Recognizing Tony Esteban, she waited, planning to say hello when he passed the fence. Tony was a great guy with a tremendous amount of talent and high hopes of entering the Olympics someday. It was obvious that he was willing to go to the wall for his dream, concentrating hard on performance and speed.

When Tony drew near, Elizabeth waved and called out a greeting.

Tony smiled at her and waved back, his dark eyes sparkling with energy and great expectations, but he didn't break his stride.

"Flirting with other guys when I'm not around, huh?" teased a masculine voice from behind her.

Elizabeth turned to see Todd standing there. "Of course," she said with a toss of her head

151

and a mischievous grin. "Tony's pretty cute, and besides, you never know when you might need a spare boyfriend."

Todd narrowed his eyes at her, pretending to be suspicious. "Jessica, is that you posing as Elizabeth?"

Elizabeth laughed. Todd took her hand as they walked into the school building. "You know," Todd said, "Tony's our best runner by far. From what I hear, he's got what it takes to be a professional athlete."

*Will Tony Esteban allow anything to stand in the way of his dream? Find out in Sweet Valley High #77,* **CHEATING TO WIN.**

# LOOKIN' COOL IN YOUR — SWEET VALLEY™ SUNGLASSES

Reading books is one of the coolest things you can do. But you'll be even cooler in your awesome new SWEET VALLEY™ SUNGLASSES. All SWEET VALLEY™ SUNGLASSES give UV protection, and the frames are made of durable, impact resistant plastic. The glasses have incredible COLOR MAGIC frames that actually change color in sunlight, and each pair of glasses will be imprinted with the SWEET VALLEY™ insignia. SWEET VALLEY™ SUNGLASSES are totally cool and totally free to the first 10,000 kids we hear from who've purchased a SWEET VALLEY™ book containing this coupon. If you want a pair fill in the coupon below (no photocopies or facsimilies allowed), cut it out and send it to:

**SWEET VALLEY™ SUNGLASSES
BANTAM BOOKS, YOUNG READERS MARKETING, Dept. IG**
**666 Fifth Avenue, New York, New York 10103**

SVH-8  6/91